FOSTER'S WAR

CAROLYN REEDER

AN
APPLE
PAPERBACK

SCHOLASTIC INC.
New York Toronto London Auckland Sydney
Mexico City New Delhi Hong Kong

AUTHOR'S NOTE

During the Second World War, Americans commonly referred to their Japanese enemies as "the Japs." After more than half a century of peace with Japan, the word "Jap" is considered disrespectful. You will find it in the dialogue in this book, however, because Foster's war is World War II.

ISBN: 0-590-09856-X

Copyright © 1998 by Carolyn Reeder.
Cover painting © 1998 by Tim O'Brien.
All rights reserved. Published by Scholastic Inc.
SCHOLASTIC, APPLE PAPERBACKS, and associated logos are trademarks and/or registered trademarks of Scholastic Inc.

24 23 22 21 20 19 18 17 16 15 14   10/0

Printed in the U.S.A.   40

First Scholastic Trade paperback printing, November 2000

Cover design by Elizabeth B. Parisi
Interior design by David Caplan

For my first readers—
Anne, Barbara, and Ellen

Foster lay on the top bunk, listening to the scream of sirens, hoping six-year-old Ricky wouldn't wake up but knowing that he would. He felt the bunk below him shake, heard his younger brother on the ladder.

"Hey, Foss." Ricky's face was so close to his that Foster could feel his brother's breath in the darkness.

"It's not an air raid, Ricky. It's fire engines—you can hear the bells."

Ricky listened, then said, "Maybe the bombs started a fire. Maybe they were firebombs, like the man on the radio told—"

"That was in Germany, and it was our side that dropped them. Besides, we'd have heard the air-raid siren if it was the Japs."

"And then we would all get under the kitchen table, right?"

Foster tried to picture the whole Simmons family huddled under the table in their nightclothes. Well, not

1

the *whole* family. Father would have grabbed his white air-raid warden's helmet and gone out to make sure not a sliver of light shone from any of the houses in the neighborhood. And thanks to Father, Mel had left school to join the Army Air Force long before Pearl Harbor. So it would just be himself, Ricky, Mom, and his fifteen-year-old sister, Evelyn. The Evil Lynn.

"Right, Foster? Right?" There was a note of panic in Ricky's voice now.

"Right," Foster said quickly.

"Tell me again why we'd have to get under the table."

Foster sighed. "Because it's the safest place to be. If the roof collapsed, it would fall on the table and you'd be sitting there underneath, safe and sound." He wished Ricky had never seen those civil defense pamphlets that told what to do in case of an air raid.

"Then the lower bunk would be pretty safe, wouldn't it? Listen, Foss, why don't you sleep down there with me?"

"'Cause I'm safe right where I am! Go on back to bed, Ricky. The sirens have stopped now."

"But—"

"Shh! Do you want to wake Father?"

Ricky was back on his bunk in a flash, and Foster wondered how many kids were more afraid of their fathers than of an air raid. *This is station WAR in San Diego, and we're interviewing eleven-year-old Foster*

Simmons. Tell me, Foster, which are you more afraid of, an air raid or your father?

Foster wondered what he would say if he had to face that question in real life. Caught up in his fantasy now, he frowned. With civil defense plane spotters always on duty and anti-aircraft guns trained on the sky, Jap pilots probably wouldn't get through, he thought. And if they did, the barrage balloons floating blimplike above the city would stop them. But Father was a different story. Father was right here, right now.

We're waiting for your answer, Foster.

He couldn't tell the truth and embarrass his whole family—not to mention get the punishment of his life—but he'd never been a convincing liar. He wouldn't have to lie, Foster thought, grinning. He'd just say, "Mister, that's such a dopey question I'm not going to bother to answer it."

Foster's grin faded as he stared into the darkness and thought about the war, about how much his life had changed since the war began—or rather, since the United States had joined in the fighting. "Since December 7, 1941," Foster whispered. "Only a few months ago . . ."

CHAPTER
1

Foster was so intent on the hole he was digging that he barely noticed the warmth of the California afternoon or the blare of a radio coming from the alley where his older brother was washing the car. But when he straightened up to rest his back, the catchy rhythm of "Chattanooga Choo-Choo" caught Foster's ear, and he grinned. With Mel home on leave, it was almost like old times, he thought.

But his smile faded as he studied his hole and admitted that it still looked more like a hole than a pond for the goldfish he planned to buy with his allowance. "Nothing but a hole," he muttered. And not a very deep one, either—more like a bowl than a pond. He squatted down to scoop and pat more dirt in place to raise the edges, his mind idling in neutral until a voice snapped him back into gear.

"Honestly, Foster! Aren't you a bit old to be playing in the dirt?"

Foster didn't bother to look up. Evelyn's tanned bare legs and painted toenails were more than he wanted to see of her. He finished patting a rim of earth into place around the edge of his hole and then, hardly aware that his sister had left, he carefully packed down the dirt. His pond hadn't turned out like he had planned, but it would have to do, he decided, looking at it critically. Now he had to figure out a way to keep it from leaking.

Plaster of paris. That might work, and he had a sack of it in the back of his closet, left over from the project he'd done for school last month. Foster thought of the volcano he'd built, remembered how impressed the kids had been when he'd made it erupt. But the effect hadn't lasted very long. Pretty soon he was "Foster Child" again.

Reminding himself of his rule never to think about school on weekends, Foster started toward the shed for a bucket he could use to mix the plaster of paris. With a little luck, he'd be finished and have that bucket put away before Father even knew it was gone.

Foster was coming out of the shed when he saw his mother open the back door. "Hi, Mom!" he called. "Come see what I'm making."

His mother didn't answer, and something about the way she moved put Foster on guard even before he saw her face. "What's wrong, Mom!" he asked. "Is Father mad? What did I do now?"

His mother shook her head. "It's not anything you did this time." She took a deep breath and said, "It's war, son. The Japanese have bombed our naval base at Pearl Harbor."

Foster stared at her. "Where's that?" he asked in a small voice. It couldn't be anywhere near San Diego if he'd never heard of it, could it?

"It's on one of the Hawaiian Islands."

Relieved, Foster closed his eyes and pictured the world map on the wall of his classroom, the map he studied while he was waiting his turn to diagram a sentence at the board. There they were—the Hawaiian Islands, United States territory in the Pacific. Tiny pink specks on the blue of the ocean. Plenty far away from California, he thought.

But even farther from Japan. Foster's eyes popped open, and his heart began to pound. "Do you think *we're* going to be bombed?"

"Come on inside and listen to the news," Mom said over her shoulder as she started back to the house. "I'll toss out an old towel so you can clean up at the hose before you come in."

Trying to ignore the fact that his mother hadn't answered his question, Foster headed for the spigot. How could the Japs be dropping bombs on American ships while two thousand miles away he was having a perfectly ordinary afternoon? Maybe it was all a mistake, he thought as he hosed off his arms and legs. Maybe the announcer really said that someday the Japanese *might* bomb Pearl Harbor. Maybe when he went inside Mom would tell him not to worry, that she'd misunderstood. Foster took a deep breath and began to feel better.

A few minutes later, he slipped into the living room where his family was listening to the radio. Father was leaning forward in his chair, feet planted solidly on the patterned rug. His huge hands rested on his thighs, the elbows pointing out, and his stocky body was tensed as though he might leap to his feet any moment.

Across the room, Evelyn sat on the arm of the sofa, half leaning against her mother, and Ricky was pressed as close to Mom as he could get. It wasn't a mistake, Foster thought, feeling his stomach tighten. It was true.

Mel! Where was Mel? Before anyone noticed Foster, he backed out of the room and dashed outside. Yes, Mel was sitting in the driver's seat, listening to the car radio, his bucket and sponge abandoned and soapsuds drying on the hood. Foster climbed into the passenger seat just as the announcer said, "I repeat: All active-duty service-men on leave are to return to their bases immediately. Stay tuned to this station for more—"

"But we were going bowling tomorrow night!" Foster's voice rose, drowning out the announcer, and his sentence ended in an embarrassing squeak.

But Mel didn't laugh. He just clicked off the radio and said, "You'll have to finish the car for me while I pack, kiddo."

"What do you think is going to happen?" Foster asked.

"I think I might get a chance to help make those Japs wish they'd never heard of Pearl Harbor," Mel said grimly, but then he smiled and ruffled his younger brother's sun-bleached hair. "Don't worry, kid—the U.S. Army Air Force will take care of the Japs." Mel climbed out of the car, and Foster watched him stride purposefully toward the house. Even when he was wearing jeans, Mel looked like a serviceman.

Talking into his fist as though it were a microphone, Foster announced, "Melvin Simmons was called back to his base today because of the bombing of Pearl Harbor. Young Simmons, who is completing his training as a member of a bomber crew, is hoping for a chance to avenge the—"

With no warning, the car door was wrenched open, and Foster found himself staring into his father's angry face.

"Don't you know I have to drive your brother to the bus station? Get out here and start hosing the soap off the car!"

Foster slid across the front seat and slipped out the door on the driver's side. He grabbed the hose and had just turned the nozzle to let the water spray the hood when his father bellowed, "Hey! Watch it!"

Oh, no. Oh, *no*! Foster didn't breathe until he saw

that his father had jumped back in time to avoid being splashed.

"What's the matter with you, anyway? Can't you ever do anything right?" Red faced, Mr. Simmons glared across the hood at Foster for a moment before he went back to the house.

Foster drew a few shaky breaths to calm himself and then muttered resentfully, "I can do a lot of things, right, not that he'd ever notice." He adjusted the nozzle and silently continued his broadcast. *While Mel Simmons was packing, his eleven-year-old brother, Foster, narrowly escaped harm when a carelessly aimed hose resulted in an explosion. More about that after this word from our sponsor.*

CHAPTER

2

"What's the hurry, Rick?" Foster asked, running a few steps to catch up with his brother as they set off for school the next morning.

Ricky walked faster still and didn't answer, but at the drone of a plane in the distance, a look of terror crossed his face and he cried, "Run for your life, Foss! It's the Japs!"

Foster caught up with his brother just before they reached the corner. Grabbing the back of the little boy's shirt, he yelled, "If you get hit by a car, you won't have to worry about being bombed!" Then, seeing the fearful expression on his brother's face, he said, "Heck, you don't have to worry about it anyhow, Rick. Pearl Harbor's a long way from here."

Actually, it was a long way from just about anywhere, Foster thought as he visualized the map again, but that hadn't seemed to make any difference. If the Japs would attack a naval base and airfield, they might bomb a city that was known for its shipyards and aircraft factory, too—a city like San Diego. Foster felt a prickly sensation in his scalp.

"Can't we walk just a little faster?" Ricky begged.

"You want to catch up to Victor?" Foster pointed to a sturdy dark-haired boy walking some distance ahead of them. Victor was a more immediate—and surer—threat than Japanese bombers.

Two little girls ran out of the house they were passing and called, "Can we walk with you and your big brother, Rick?"

Their mother, still in her housecoat, followed them to the sidewalk and said apologetically, "I hope you don't mind, Foster, but the twins are still a bit unsettled after the bombing yesterday."

"I guess a lot of the little kids are," he said, earning a hurt look from his brother. "You girls stick with Ricky, and I'll be your fearless leader," he said. "Stay behind me, and don't come too close, 'cause I'll be scouting ahead to make sure everything's safe." The last thing he needed was for the kids to see him walking with a bunch of first graders.

After they all crossed the avenue a block before the school, Foster looked down at the younger children and asked, "You want to run the rest of the way?" And when three heads nodded, he said, "Go on, then." He watched them sprint down the sidewalk ahead of him.

Today, instead of being involved in games on the playground, most of the students were clustered against the building, and Foster wondered what made them think they were safer there. Hadn't they seen the photographs of ruined buildings in London after the German air raids?

To take his mind off bombed-out homes, Foster scanned the playground, looking for Jimmy Osaki, knowing he would be off somewhere by himself. Where was he, anyhow? Foster sighed and jammed his hands in his pockets. He wished the bell would ring.

"Hey, Foster Child—I asked you something." It was Michael, the best athlete in the fifth grade. "Is your dad joining up?"

"No, but my brother's in the Army Air Force," Foster said proudly.

"What about *your* dad, Wilbur?" Victor asked, and then all the others began taunting the heavyset boy slouched against the building. "Yeah, Wilbur, what about *your* dad?"

Foster turned away. He wished the kids would lay off—it wasn't Wilbur's fault that he had a series of "uncles" instead of a father. Besides, Foster didn't want to see the hurt and anger on Wilbur's face. Wilbur should practice in front of a mirror until he could keep his face from showing how he felt. Life had been easier for *him* since he'd done that.

"Hey, Foster Child! Where's your slant-eyed friend today?" Victor called.

Foster shrugged and turned away. He hated it when the other kids called Jimmy "slant-eyes" or "dirty Jap," hated Victor's ugly tone of voice. Jimmy was as much an American as the rest of them, even if his parents did come here from Japan. Uh-oh. That was why Jimmy wasn't at school today. Foster stared at the gravel surface of the playground and wished he'd never heard of Pearl Harbor.

At last the bell rang, and for once, everyone seemed more than ready to go inside. Foster's spirits sank even lower when he walked into the classroom and saw Mrs. Jackson plugging in a radio. The one at home had been on ever since the news broke, and he was sick of hearing the same thing over and over again. He just wanted to forget about the bombing, to forget that Mel's leave had been cut short.

"Good morning, boys and girls," Mrs. Jackson said when they were all in their seats. "I can see that you're all wondering why I brought the radio. You've probably heard that President Roosevelt is making a speech to Congress today, and I thought we should listen since it's bound to be a historic occasion."

Pam, the most popular girl in the class, raised her hand, but without waiting to be called on she burst out, "My father says the president's going to declare war on Japan—and maybe on Germany, too."

Above the din of voices, Mrs. Jackson said, "We'll

find out all about that when we hear the president's speech, boys and girls, but right now it's time for our opening exercises." She picked up the Bible from its place on her desk and stood waiting for the clamor to subside.

After Mrs. Jackson read a chapter from the Bible and everyone repeated the Lord's Prayer, the class stood for the pledge to the flag. Foster put his right hand over his heart, and as he recited the familiar words, he thought about what they meant: allegiance . . . nation . . . liberty. He was still musing over the words when he noticed that all around him hands waved wildly in the air.

Mrs. Jackson shook her head and said, "I'm choosing our song this morning, and it will be 'God Bless America.'" She gave the pitch, and as the class began to sing, Foster felt a swell of something he couldn't quite describe. By the time they had sung the final "God bless America, my home sweet home," he thought his heart would burst, and he saw that Mrs. Jackson's eyes were moist.

The class sat down and waited without a sound while their teacher straightened the pile of books on her desk and then lined up her ruler and several pencils along the right-hand side. At last she looked up and said, "Boys and girls, you have all heard the news of the attack on our naval base yesterday. You all know that our country has no choice but to join in the war that has been raging in Europe and Asia. We are facing difficult times, as a nation and as families and individuals."

Mrs. Jackson paused for a moment to glance around the room and meet the thirty-nine pairs of eyes that were glued to her face. "But meanwhile," she went on, "each of us has a job to do. Mine is to teach, yours is to learn, and we are going to try to keep things as normal as possible here in our classroom. Do you understand?" Heads nodded solemnly, and Mrs. Jackson said, "Good. Please get out your reading books and workbooks."

Foster had finished the dull reader assigned to his group months ago and had zipped through the multiple-choice lessons in his workbook, circling or underlining answers at random so he could answer honestly when Mrs. Jackson asked if he'd finished it. He'd noticed long ago that she looked to see if the pages were done but didn't really check the work of students who were good readers.

Foster rummaged in his desk for his library book and opened it to the page he'd marked with a scrap of paper. This was his favorite part of the school day. But he hadn't been reading long when he gradually became aware that his teacher was speaking to the class. ". . . tell your own children about how you heard President Roosevelt's historic speech when you were in fifth grade."

Mrs. Jackson turned on the radio, and Foster frowned. How could she expect them to hear with all that static? No, not static—applause. He was actually hearing all the senators and representatives clapping, just like any other audience. And then Foster heard the president's voice, and it was as clear as if he were in the classroom and not three thousand miles away. "Yesterday, December 7, 1941, a date which will live in infamy, the United States of America was suddenly and deliberately attacked by naval and air forces of the Empire of Japan."

Empire? Foster hadn't known there were still empires—he'd thought they were from the days of fairy tales. He wondered if the Japanese emperor wore rich-looking robes like men did in the paintings at Jimmy Osaki's house. Jimmy and his parents were probably listening now, too, gathered around the table in their spick-and-span kitchen. Probably everyone in the whole country who had a radio was listening.

Suddenly realizing that *he* wasn't listening, Foster turned his mind back to the radio in time to hear the president say, "I ask that the Congress declare that since the unprovoked and dastardly attack by Japan on Sunday, December 7, a state of war has existed between the United States and the Japanese Empire."

A state of war, Foster thought. And this time yesterday he'd never even heard of Pearl Harbor. This time yesterday, it was the *Germans* that people worried about. The Nazis.

Mrs. Jackson turned off the radio, and Michael asked, "What's going to happen now?"

"Congress will approve the president's declaration of war," Mrs. Jackson said. Ignoring the hands waving in front of her, she added, "I think this is a good time to tell you about how our government works—about the separation of powers and all the 'checks and balances' that are built into our Constitution."

As Mrs. Jackson turned to the board and picked up a piece of chalk, Foster sat up straighter. This was going to be a lot more interesting than subjects and predicates.

The board was covered with a diagram showing the three branches of government by the time a slim, gray-haired woman came into the room. It was the principal, Miss Cook. "I'm sorry to interrupt, boys and girls, but I have something very serious to discuss with you," she said.

It must be really serious for the principal to come out of her office like this, Foster thought. He sat up even straighter.

"In a few days," Miss Cook continued, "we will have our first air-raid drill. When you hear the alarm ring, you will line up and follow your teacher into the hall-way and sit down against the wall. You will sit there quietly until the all-clear signal, and then you will follow your teacher back to your classroom. Are there any questions? Very well. Remember, I'm depending on your cooperation."

The moment the door shut behind the principal, almost every hand was raised, and Wilbur was leaning so far across his desk that Foster was sure he'd have fallen forward if the desks and chairs hadn't been bolted to the floor. But Mrs. Jackson called on Sally, the girl who sat in front of Foster.

"Does this mean we're going to be bombed?" Sally asked, her voice trembling.

"Does having fire drills mean the school's going to burn down?" Mrs. Jackson asked gently. Sally shook her head, and Mrs. Jackson said, "Well, the air-raid drills shouldn't worry you any more than the fire drills do." She looked at the sea of hands waving in front of her and said, "I don't know any more about this than you do, boys and girls, but it really shouldn't be very complicated, should it? We'll just file into the hall, one row at a time, and sit down quietly. I want you to be on your best behavior to show Miss Cook what a fine class you are and to be a good example for the younger children."

Ignoring the hands that continued to wave, Mrs. Jackson glanced at the clock and said, "Goodness, it's time for our spelling pretest."

Foster would have preferred to hear more about how the government worked, but he dutifully got out a sheet of paper and wrote his name in the top right-hand corner. Below that, where they were supposed to put the date, he carefully wrote, "Day of Infamy + 1."

All that day, Foster found his eyes straying to the empty seat two rows to the left, and as soon as he got home he asked his mother if he could go over to Jimmy Osaki's house.

"Be careful crossing streets," Mrs. Simmons warned. "I worry that someday you'll step in front of a car while you're thinking about something else."

Foster didn't want to think about the time he almost did just that. "There aren't very many streets to cross," he said as he headed for the door.

The afternoon sun was warm on his back, and birds were singing in the flowering trees—just like before the bombing. Foster tried to pretend that nothing had happened, that it had all been one of those complicated dreams that seem so real, but for once his imagination failed him. He had an uneasy feeling that nothing would ever be quite the same again.

"School sure was different today," he muttered, and not just because Jimmy was absent for the first time in the year and a half they'd known each other. Jimmy. How must it feel to look different from everyone else?

To look like the enemy? It must be awful when people didn't like you because you looked different. It was bad enough when they didn't like you because you *were* different. Would Jimmy have been his friend if they hadn't both been outcasts? Not outcasts, exactly—he searched for the word—misfits. Now, though, Jimmy had become an outcast because of the bombing.

Yes, Foster decided, they would have been friends no matter what, because they both liked to do things the other kids weren't interested in. Things like playing chess, and collecting stamps, and doing experiments with Jimmy's chemistry set. Reading comic books was just about the only thing they did that all the other kids did, too.

Foster passed the sign that said CITY LIMITS and realized he was almost there. He liked visiting Jimmy, liked the stark neatness of the Osakis' small home, liked the strangeness of it—especially the way no one wore shoes inside.

The lane that led to the house passed between fields of berries, and it was marked by a sign that said OSAKI FRUIT AND BERRY FARM. Foster had always admired the graceful lettering on the sign and wished he could write like that.

But today when he glanced up at the sign, Foster stopped and stared. Scrawled across it in red paint were the words KILL THE DIRTY JAPS, and droplets of paint had been splattered all around the words. No wonder Jimmy hadn't come to school! He must have thought— And he would have been right, Foster realized, remembering the hatred in Victor's voice when he'd asked about "your slant-eyed friend." He began to run.

"Hey, Jimmy!" he called as he neared the house and saw his friend sitting on the front steps. Foster stopped short when he saw Jimmy's face. "Jimmy?" The other boy looked different, somehow. "I missed you at school," Foster said, feeling awkward, as though he were making conversation with someone at a bus stop instead of talking to his best friend. His only friend.

"I'm not going to that school anymore," Jimmy said, his voice flat.

"Won't your father make you go?"

Jimmy's face contorted, and he choked out, "They took him away. Last night."

"Took him away?" Foster echoed. "But who—"

"The FBI! Because he was a member of Sons of Japan. They wouldn't believe it's just a social club, like the Rotary."

His voice almost a whisper, Foster asked, "Did they take him to—um, to—"

"To jail? Yes, they took him to jail."

Foster had to look away from his friend's anguished face. "Gosh, Jimmy. I'm really sorry." Kind, gentle Mr. Osaki in jail?

"If you're sorry because white people like you put my father in jail, how do you think I feel that yellow people like me bombed Pearl Harbor?" When Foster drew back, Jimmy said, "Don't tell me you've never heard of the dreaded Yellow Peril."

Foster didn't know what to say, so he just sat down on the step next to Jimmy. The other boy's hurt and anger seemed to hang in the air, separating them like an invisible curtain. Jimmy wasn't really yellow any more than *he* was really white, Foster thought, stealing a glance at the arm next to his. The Negroes who had come West to find work weren't really black, either, and nobody he knew was the color of the "flesh" crayon in the Crayola box. Words should mean what they say, he thought.

Finally Foster said, "If you want, I can bring your assignments over every afternoon so you don't fall behind."

"My mom's sending me to stay with my aunt's family. They live in a Japanese neighborhood, so I'll be able to go to school with other *Nisei*. Other Japanese Americans," Jimmy explained when he saw Foster's frown. "Mom's going to stay here and run the berry gardens till they let my dad come home. If they ever do," he added bitterly.

The boys sat on the step, not speaking, as the shadows grew longer and longer. Foster could hardly believe that Jimmy was going away, that they wouldn't be at school together anymore. It was seeing Jimmy every day that made school bearable.

"I'd better get on home," Foster said at last, "or else Mom's going to worry that I've been hit by a car or something." Jimmy nodded without looking at him, and Foster asked hesitantly, "You going to write to me?"

After a long silence, Jimmy shrugged and said, "Maybe."

"Well, bye," Foster said. He walked down the lane without looking back, and he forced himself to look straight ahead when he passed the sign on the road. But all the sad way home, he could see it in his mind's eye—the hateful words and the splattered drops of paint that ran like blood.

CHAPTER

3

oster and Ricky were listening to the radio and drawing war planes when they heard their sister wail, "Mommmmm! Mom, those boys have been into my things!" Foster turned to his brother, but Ricky's face mirrored his own surprise. "Come on, Rick," he said, "we'd better go defend ourselves against the Evil Lynn."

"—spilled all over my bureau, and what's worse, the lacquered box is gone, and it's my favorite thing!" Turning to her brothers as they came into the kitchen, Evelyn cried, "How dare you go in my room! And what have you done with my—"

But before she could finish, Mrs. Simmons said, "It was your father, Evelyn."

"*Father* went in my room and dumped out all my jewelry?"

Foster grinned at the image of his father, wrapped in a villain's cloak that he held across his face, tiptoeing into Evelyn's room and reaching for her lacquered jewelry box with a sinister chuckle. No, with a hollow chuckle, Foster thought, or maybe a hollow laugh.

Mrs. Simmons took a deep breath and said, "After your father heard the casualty figures from Pearl Harbor last night, he went though the house looking for anything that had been made in Japan. He didn't find much, but what he found he— Well, he destroyed what he found. I'm truly sorry about your jewelry box, Evelyn."

"Oh, Mom! Even your teapot? The pretty one that was a wedding present?"

"The teapot's safe," Mom said. "When he smashed the vase I'd filled with flowers from the yard, I knew what was coming, and I found a safe place for it."

"Couldn't you have saved my jewelry box, too?" Evelyn asked wistfully.

Mom sighed. "To tell you the truth, Evelyn, your jewelry box was the farthest thing from my mind right then."

Foster and Ricky exchanged glances. So that was what had been going on after they went to bed the night before, Foster thought. He had heard raised voices and the sound of something breaking and had huddled under the covers pretending to be asleep when Father stormed down the hall.

Father had never actually hit any of them, but it was

easy to forget that when he was in one of his rages. Last night Foster had decided that Father must be checking Evelyn's room for cigarettes while she was rehearsing for the choir concert at church.

"Come on, Rick," Foster said. "Since Evelyn isn't going to apologize for accusing us falsely, we might as well go back and listen to our program."

"Well, it's the kind of thing you'd be likely to do," Evelyn said sullenly.

"Now, be fair, Evelyn. It's been months since the boys were in your room, and that was Mel's doing."

Foster pushed Ricky down the hall ahead of him, choking back laughter. He would never forget how angry his sister had been when Mel short-sheeted her bed. Or how after Mel had promised never to do it again, he'd showed the two of them how to fold the bottom half of the top sheet toward the head of the bed so there would be no room for Evelyn to stretch out her legs when she climbed in.

What a rage she had flown into! It was a good thing Father was on the night shift at the aircraft factory then, or all four of them would have been in big trouble, Foster thought, grinning at the memory of Mel's protests of innocence.

"Where's your mother?"

"Huh?" Foster gave a start when he saw his father standing just inside the front door. "She's in the kitchen," he said.

But Ricky was already hollering, "Mom! He's home."

Mrs. Simmons hurried to meet her husband and take his lunch box. "I didn't hear you come in, Horace," she said after she gave him a kiss on the cheek. "Dinner will be ready by the time you are."

"Roosevelt's addressing the nation in a couple of minutes, and I want to hear what he has to say."

Mrs. Simmons glanced at her watch and said, "I'll put the oven on low and we'll all listen."

Father turned on the radio in time for them to hear the familiar voice of the president say, "We are now in this war! We are all in it—all the way. Every single man, woman and child is a partner in the most tremendous undertaking of our American history. We must share together the bad news and the good news, the defeats and the victories—the changing fortunes of war."

Every child, even! A chill went down Foster's spine. He was trying to concentrate on the president's words when his mother made an impatient sound and left the room.

Ricky hurried after her, calling, "Mom! How come you aren't going to listen anymore, Mom? Hey, Mom!"

"Quiet!" Father roared, and he launched into a tirade that drowned out the president's words and ended with ". . . kid doesn't have half the sense he was born with!"

Foster sat as still as possible and stared at the floor. He'd learned long ago that when Father was angry, it didn't pay to catch his eye. It wasn't until the cultured voice of the president could be heard again that Foster began to relax. Looking up, he saw that Father had leaned back in his chair and closed his eyes as he listened.

Evelyn held a finger to her lips and tiptoed out of the room, and Foster followed her.

When they all sat down to dinner a short time later, Mr. Simmons turned to his wife. In a disapproving voice he said, "I don't see what was so important it couldn't wait while you listened to your president."

"You mean the president who promised that our sons wouldn't be sent into foreign wars?" she asked.

"It's not a foreign war any longer," Father argued. "When those Japs bombed—"

Mom covered her ears. "Just ask the blessing, Horace," she said sharply. "I'd like to eat before the food gets cold."

Automatically, Foster bowed his head. All Father could think about was "those Japs," and all Mom could think about was how Mel would soon be in the war. *He* thought about both. He was afraid of the Japs, and he'd be afraid for Mel once he was overseas, but right now he just missed him.

"*Fos*ter!"

Foster's eyes popped open and he reached for the plate his father was holding. When he passed it on to

Ricky, he noticed that it was one of Mel's favorite meals. Mom had expected him to be here for dinner tonight, Foster thought, stealing a glance at her. "Good dinner, Mom," he said impulsively. That's what Mel would have said if he'd been home.

CHAPTER
4

H e's here, Mom," Ricky called when the old Plymouth pulled up in front of the house the next Monday evening.

"And it looks like he's in a good mood," Foster added as his father climbed out of the car. Turning away from the window, Foster watched Mom hurry to meet his father, smoothing her dark hair and her dress as she went.

"Well, Ruby," Father said, handing her his lunch box, "I'll have you know you're looking at your neighborhood warden." He turned to his sons and barked, "Go bring in the stuff on the backseat."

The brothers raced to the car and found a white helmet with WARDEN stenciled on the front, a whistle, an official-looking book, and a rubber-banded stack of pamphlets. "'What to do in case of an air raid,'" Foster read.

"What *do* we do, Foss?" Ricky asked in a small voice.

Foster pulled out the top pamphlet and skimmed

through it. "It says to lie down under a table," he said, "and every family is supposed to have an emergency supply of food and water." When Foster saw a worried frown on Ricky's face, he reached for the helmet and set it on his brother's head. Grinning at the way it covered half the little boy's face, he hung the whistle around his own neck.

"Let's go," he said as he handed his brother the book and picked up the pamphlets.

Ricky looked at the book's title and read, "'In— In—something for N—something War-dens.'"

"'Instructions for Neighborhood Wardens,'" Foster read.

"What's a warden, anyway?"

Foster slammed the car door and said, "Well, a prison warden's the person in charge of a prison, so I guess—"

He was interrupted by a shout from the porch. "What's taking you two so long? Get on in here."

The boys sprinted up the sidewalk, but when Foster saw his father glowering at them from the porch, he wished he could run the other way. Father grabbed each boy by an arm and propelled them inside. He tore the helmet from Ricky's head and almost ripped off Foster's ear when he jerked away the whistle on its lanyard.

"These are government property," Father raged. "Don't you ever let me see you touch them again!" Reaching for the stack of civil defense pamphlets and the book, he snapped, "And what have you done with the armband? If you lost it while you were fooling around, I'll—"

"We'll see if it's still in the car," Foster said, bolting out the door with Ricky at his heels.

They found it on the floor of the backseat—a white armband with the letters CD inside a triangle—and raced back to the house with it. Father was waiting for them, filling the doorway. "You'd better be glad you found that," he declared.

The boys followed him to the kitchen, where he took his place at the head of the table. As Foster slipped past to reach his own seat, he glanced at Mel's empty chair opposite him and then concentrated on watching Evelyn help her mother place the platters and bowls of food in front of Father.

As soon as everyone was seated, Father bowed his head and said, "Lord, we are thankful for the food we are about to receive. Bless it to our use and us in thy service. Amen. So as I was saying, being an air-raid warden is a big responsibility, but each of us has to do his part. *Fos*ter!"

Foster gave a start and opened his eyes. "Yessir!"

"Did you hear what I said?"

"Yessir! 'Lord, we are thankful for—' "

"Not the grace, boy! What I said about your doing your part. After dinner, I want you and your brother to deliver those pamphlets for me. And tell everybody that

I'm air-raid warden and I'll be coming around to inspect and make sure not a crack of light shows around their blackout curtains."

As Foster ate, he imagined a high wall enclosing the neighborhood, a wall with no gates, and his father in the central tower, scanning the area for telltale cracks of light. A real prison warden probably stayed in his office, Foster thought, but then he would have more to worry about than—

"Would you like some more meat loaf, dear?"

Foster was about to say yes when he saw that Ricky was sitting on the edge of his seat, waiting for him to finish. If Rick fell off his chair again tonight, Father would— "No, thanks, Mom. May Ricky and I please be excused?"

A moment later, Foster carefully shut the screen door behind them so it wouldn't slam. "How do you want to do this, Rick? We'd finish sooner if each of us takes one side of the street."

"Let's go together, then."

Any excuse to stay out of Father's way, Foster thought as they started down the walk. Well, almost any. *He* certainly wouldn't have quit school and joined the army like Mel had, not even to get away from Father for good.

Ricky rang the bell at the house next door. He was about to ring again when they heard slow footsteps approaching, and at last their elderly neighbor stepped out onto the porch.

Foster handed him a pamphlet and said, "Hi, Mr. Green. Ricky and I are delivering civil defense literature. You're supposed to read this so you'll know what to do in case of an air raid. Our father's the air-raid warden, and he'll be checking to make sure your blackout curtains don't let any light show through."

"That's so the Japs won't drop bombs on us," Ricky explained. "If they don't see any lights, they won't know they're flying over a city."

The old man nodded and said, "Since I have no blackout curtains, I will simply keep my lights turned off. It will not matter, because I no longer read at night now that my sight is poor."

"Let me read you the notice, then," Foster said, and he took the pamphlet back and began to read.

When he finished, Mr. Green thanked him and said, "But now you must hurry with the rest of your deliveries. Your father will be impatient if you do not return when he expects."

The boys gave pamphlets to the other neighbors on their side of the street, then crossed to the other side. Foster felt his steps begin to lag as they approached the house on the corner. Maybe Victor's mother would come to the door, or maybe his five-year-old brother, Sandy.

Ricky rang the bell, and when Foster heard the thud of running footsteps inside, he knew it was Victor.

"What do you want, Foster Child? We're eating."

"Give your mom this civil defense pamphlet and tell her that my father's the neighborhood air-raid warden. He's going to make sure no light shines through your blackout curtains." Maybe the light in Victor's room would show, and—

Victor took the pamphlet and said, "How come you get to pass these out, Foster Child?"

Crossing his fingers, Foster said, "Hadn't you heard? I'm the neighborhood leader of California Youth for the War Effort."

A look of respect mingled with envy crossed Victor's face, and he said, "Okay, Foster. I'll give this to my mom right away."

As the brothers walked away, Ricky asked, "Can I join Youth for the War Effort? Can I, Foss?"

Foster wasn't surprised that Ricky had taken his sarcastic remark at face value, but Victor? "We can talk about that later," he stalled, enjoying the idea of being a leader, "but right now we have to give out the rest of these pamphlets."

Foster pulled the covers off the bottom bunk and rolled Ricky onto the floor. "Get up, Rick. It's breakfast time," he said, and then he headed for the kitchen, looking forward to the few minutes he had alone with Mom each morning.

"Smells good," he said as his mother added strips of bacon to the pancakes she had flipped onto his plate.

"You know what I found out last night when we gave Mr. Green his pamphlet?" Foster asked as he sat down and reached for the syrup. "He doesn't have blackout curtains, so he's just going to sit in the dark. He says it won't matter since he can't see well enough to read anymore."

Mom cut an orange in half, pressed it onto the juicer, and rested her weight on it as she turned it back and forth. "Well, I'm glad you read him the notice," she said. "I hate to think what would have happened if light had been pouring from his windows during a blackout. You know how impatient your father can be with older people."

Mel would have said, "I know how impatient he can be with *younger* people," but Foster contented himself with thinking it. He didn't want to make his mother feel bad.

"If the dime store still has that black fabric," Mrs. Simmons mused, "it wouldn't take me long to stitch up some curtains for Mr. Green. I'll go over later this morning and talk to him about it."

A sense of well-being settled over Foster. He liked the way his mom always took charge, the way she looked after people and saw to it that things went smoothly. As smoothly as possible, anyway . . .

Half an hour later when Foster walked into the classroom, he saw Victor heading for him and steeled himself for whatever verbal abuse was about to come his way. But to his surprise, Victor said, "Hey, Foster, I brought back that library book you wanted to read. I already put your name on the card."

"Gee, thanks!" Foster said, reaching for the book. He'd been waiting more than three weeks for Victor to return it, sure that the other boy had checked it out just to keep him from borrowing it.

The bell rang, and everyone hurried to sit down. Foster's eyes were on the picture of the collie dog on the book jacket all during the opening exercises. He stood for the pledge of allegiance, parroting the words, then joined in the singing of a patriotic song, marking time until he could start his book.

The morning dragged on, but at last Mrs. Jackson called the "Eagles" reading group—which everyone knew was the low one—to the front of the room with their books, leaving the other two groups to work at their desks. Finally, Foster thought, reaching for his new library book. . . .

"Hey, Foster. *Foster!*"

"Huh?" Foster looked up from his book to see who had called him. To his dismay, everyone was staring at him. Again. But this time, no one was snickering or looking scornful.

Mrs. Jackson came to his rescue and said, "Victor just told us that you were chosen to be neighborhood leader of a group called California Youth for the War Effort. The class was wondering if you could tell us a little bit about the organization and its plans."

Oh, no. Oh, *no*! How was he going to get out of this? "Um, I was passing out civil defense pamphlets last night, Mrs. Jackson, so I haven't had a chance to study my leader's information kit," Foster said. "Could I tell the class tomorrow instead?"

Several of his classmates called out, "Vacation starts tomorrow, Foster," but Mrs. Jackson ignored them. "You can tell us when we come back from the Christmas holiday," she said. "And congratulations, Foster! I'm sure you'll do a fine job as a leader of California Youth for the War Effort, and I hope one of your first accomplishments will be to shorten that name to YWE."

He'd really done it now, Foster thought, slouching down in his seat. Why did Victor have to blab to the whole class about—

"Fosterrrrr!"

Foster blinked and reached for the papers Sally was waving in his face, took a sheet, and passed the rest back down the row. He saw that Mrs. Jackson had already rolled up the world map to uncover the sixteen arithmetic problems written on the blackboard. There were a few groans, a mutter of complaint, and the rustle of thirty-nine pieces of paper being folded in half again and again, then unfolded to show sixteen small rectangles, one for each problem.

Forgetting everything but the assignment on the board, Foster muttered, "Finally! Something to *do*." Something that was a challenge, or rather something that he could make into one. While his classmates began to copy the problems, he looked at the three-digit numbers in the first addition of decimals problem and calculated the sum the way Mel had taught him to. He wrote the answer and then ran his eyes down each column to check himself. Mrs. Jackson had reluctantly agreed to let him do the problems without copying them, but only as long as every answer was correct.

Ooops—off by one in the hundreds' place. Not bad, though, he thought as he erased and changed the number. If he was careful he could still match his record—all but one problem correctly solved in his head on the first try. The subtraction was easier to do by mental arithmetic, but he had to copy the multiplication and division problems and work them out.

After he quickly checked to make sure all his decimal points were in the right places, Foster turned his paper over. What a pickle he'd gotten himself into with that Youth for the War Effort remark. YWE, Mrs. Jackson had called it. He would have to tell her he'd lied, have to admit that he should have owned up instead of lying again. But how could he have done that in front of all the kids? Foster sighed. Once they found out he wasn't really a leader in the YWE, he'd never live it down.

Lightly, he drew the letters YWE on the back of his paper—block letters, with lines that led to the top right corner to show perspective, the way the art teacher had taught them when she visited the school the month before. Under the decorative heading he started to print the words the letters stood for, but then he had a better idea. You Wet Elephant, he wrote, and then, grinning, he made a list:

Yellow Weasel Eater
Yawns Will Echo
Your Worms' Eggs
Young Woolly Ears
Yo-yos Work Electrically

"That's a good one," he muttered. He was about to add Yesterday's Wise Explorer to the list when he felt someone poke him in the back.

"Come on, Foster," the girl who sat behind him whispered, "pass up the papers, for gosh sakes."

Sally, the girl in front of him, had turned around and was waiting impatiently. It was too late to erase what he'd done, so he turned his paper right side up and slipped it under the others as he handed them forward. For the first time, Foster was glad Mrs. Jackson had seated the class boy-girl-boy-girl, because if one of the boys had seen him put that paper on the bottom, he'd have pulled it out to see why. At least, that's what *he'd* have done.

Maybe Mrs. Jackson wouldn't see his doodling. Maybe she never turned the papers over, just set each one aside as she checked it. Maybe— With a jolt, Foster realized that he was the only student left in the classroom.

"Aren't you going out to recess, Foster?" Mrs. Jackson asked.

"Um, there's something I have to tell you, Mrs. Jackson. Something about the um, the YWE."

"Something about the Yellow Weasel Eater?"

Foster felt hot all over. "I'm sorry I wasted my time doodling on the back of my paper," he mumbled.

But all Mrs. Jackson said was, "Your math problems were correct, as usual."

"About the YWE," Foster said, trying again, "I'm not really the neighborhood leader for Youth for the War Effort. I made that up. There isn't any such a thing."

"Well, if there isn't, there ought to be," Mrs. Jackson said. "And since your classmates showed so much interest in this organization you made up, I think you're going to have to go ahead with what you've started."

Foster stared at her. This must be her way of punishing him for turning in messy papers and not paying attention in class, he decided, feeling betrayed. He'd thought that for once he had a teacher who liked him. Finding his voice, he said, "But everybody thinks I'm going to come in here after the holidays with a bunch of ideas from my leader's information kit!"

"Then that's what you'll have to do," Mrs. Jackson said.

"But what if I can't think of anything? They'll all laugh at me and—"

"Nonsense, Foster. You're a bright boy, and you're full of ideas. Nobody's going to laugh at you when you stand up here and tell your classmates what they can do to help their country. Now go on outside and get some fresh air and sunshine."

Foster walked into the hall and down the stairs to the boys' side of the playground as ideas whirled through his mind. This was his chance, and he was going to make the most of it. He was—

A football glanced off his shoulder and Michael yelled, "Oops! Sorry, Foster Child."

Foster ignored the burst of laughter and ran after the flopping ball. He picked it up, careful to place his fingers on the laces so it would spiral when he threw it. Concentrating, he drew his arm back until the ball was cocked behind his ear, then took a step forward and let it fly, just the way Mel had taught him to. "Perfect!" he whispered.

The boys' laughter stopped as the football spun through the air like a bullet. They scrambled backward, trying to catch it, but it sailed over the chain-link fence around the playground. Foster saw the fifth- and sixth-grade boys press their faces against the fence in disbelief. "Thank you, big brother," he whispered. Those long hours of practice had been worth it.

The recess bell rang, and Foster ran back to the building. The other boys lined up behind him, and Victor called, "Hey, Foster! Want to come over after school? I got a new football for my birthday."

Foster wasn't going to give anyone a chance to find out he couldn't throw like that unless he was standing still and had time to think about what he was doing. "Thanks anyway," he said, "but I've got to go through my information kit for the YWE."

"Need any help?" Victor asked, an eager look on his face. "I could come over tomorrow."

"I might be able to use you then," Foster said half-heartedly.

The fourth-grade teacher standing at the door announced, "No one is going into this building until the lines are absolutely silent. Stop that whispering, fifth graders."

Foster wondered what would happen if the lines never did quiet down, if every time Miss Pratt started to call a class to go inside, someone whispered. Maybe—

"And what are you grinning about, Foster Simmons?"

"I'm sorry, Miss Pratt. I didn't know you could hear that."

He was rewarded by snorts of smothered laughter behind him and by the stony look on Miss Pratt's face. Fourth grade had been the worst year of his life, thanks to her. And so far, this was probably the best day of his life, thanks to Mel.

CHAPTER
5

"M om, I'm home!" Foster ran through the house to
the kitchen, drawn by the smell of cookies bak-
ing. Christmas cookies! At least one thing would be the
same as other years in spite of the war. "Ricky's outside
with Sandy—he'll be right in," Foster added when his
mother turned from the counter with a smile.

"Have a good day?" she asked.

Foster nodded and watched her drop spoonfuls of
batter onto a cookie sheet. "Are you making those to
send to Mel?" he asked.

"A batch for him and one for us," his mother said,
and just as he had hoped she would, she added, "You
can take a couple of cookies from the cooling racks after you wash your hands."

Above the noise of water running in the sink, Foster
asked, "Can I look for something in your sewing basket
later?" His mother nodded, and he said, "I was wondering if you could make something for me after

dinner. See, I'm going to cut three letters out of cloth, and I need you to sew them onto a piece of felt."

"Do you have the felt?"

Foster nodded. He'd salvaged the leftover green felt from the Christmas project the art teacher had done with his class on her December visit to the school. He'd known it would come in handy sometime.

The holidays wouldn't be much fun with Mel gone and with everyone preoccupied with the war, Foster thought. Usually the radio played carols this time of year, but now he hardly ever heard anything but news. War news. German armies in Russia and North Africa, and the Japanese in the Pacific. It seemed like every day the Japs took over another island.

Suddenly aware that his mother was speaking to him, Foster said, "Huh?"

"I was saying that Mrs. Evans told me how envious Victor is that you were put in charge of Youth for the War Effort in this neighborhood," Mom repeated as she slid a cookie sheet into the oven.

Foster stopped with a bell-shaped cookie halfway to his mouth. "What did you say to her?"

"I told her I was very proud of you."

Foster grinned and bit into the still-warm cookie. "Thanks, Mom," he said. "That's why I want you to sew something for me. I need an armband with the letters YWE to show I'm the leader."

"Is this another one of your ideas, Foster? Like that so-called fishpond in the yard?"

He'd forgotten all about that fishpond! What if Father—

"I filled it up for you, in case you hadn't noticed," Mrs. Simmons said, "and I put the bucket back in the shed."

"Thanks, Mom," Foster said quietly, glad she wasn't going to lecture him about never finishing anything he started, never putting anything away. "But this new idea's going to work," he hurried on. "See, I'm going to organize all the kids in our class—maybe in the whole school—to do everything they can to help our country win the war."

Mom slid a bowl into the dishpan. "Do you really think the other kids will—"

"It's going to be different this time, Mom. Honest! You've got to believe me."

Mrs. Simmons smiled. "I believe you, son," she said. "Now go look in my sewing basket and pick out whatever you'd like me to use for your armband."

When Foster came back to the kitchen with a narrow strip of white satin and the green felt he'd retrieved from his closet, his mother said, "And now you can do something for me."

"Sure," Foster said, reaching for another cookie.

"I want you to take some groceries over to Mrs.

Osaki. I found out today that none of the local stores will sell to the Japanese. Some of them actually have signs in the window that say 'No Dogs or Japs.' Victor's mother told me she saw an old, old man in the pharmacy practically in tears because he couldn't buy medicine for his wife." Mrs. Simmons paused to compose herself, then said, "I got together some things for Mrs. Osaki and put them in your wagon."

"I didn't think you knew Mrs. Osaki," Foster said, surprised.

"I don't, but I know how terrible all of this must be for her.",

Foster was shocked to see his mother's eyes fill with tears. "I'll take the stuff over right now," he said, making his escape.

Bread, milk, half a dozen eggs, a box of breakfast cereal, a couple of oranges, a large box of rice with the top neatly taped down—why, this was all stuff from their own cupboards, from their own Frigidaire! Well, of course it was. Mom couldn't very well have gone out and bought it, could she? Not when she and Father sat down at the kitchen table after supper on Friday nights with a pile of receipts and accounted for everything they'd spent that week. Right down to the last nickel.

"It's a good thing she doesn't have to account for every bit of food she buys, too," Foster muttered as he pulled the wagon along the sidewalk. Father had no idea what was in the bags he loaded into the car and then carried from the car to the kitchen each week. He always parked in the grocery store lot and sat there reading the latest issue of *Life* while Mom shopped.

When Foster turned up the lane toward the Osaki house half an hour later, he saw that the vandalized sign was gone and the posts that had held it stood like a pair of orphans. He wondered if Jimmy felt a little bit like an orphan now that he was living with his aunt's family instead of with his parents, wondered if Jimmy ever thought about him. Ever missed him.

"Seems like he's been gone forever," Foster muttered as he pulled his wagon up to the house and went to ring the doorbell. His footsteps echoed as he crossed the wooden porch, and he was surprised to see that the front door was closed even though the day was warm and pleasant. Had Jimmy's mother gone to live with relatives, too? No, he could see the wash billowing on the clothesline in the side yard.

No one answered his ring, and Foster was about to go around to the kitchen door when he saw the curtain in the living room window move ever so slightly. "It's me, Foster Simmons," he called, automatically slipping off his shoes. Mrs. Jackson would have made him say "It is I," but he thought that sounded more like William Shakespeare than Foster Simmons.

The door opened, and Mrs. Osaki pulled him inside

and hugged him. After a moment of shocked surprise, he self-consciously hugged her back. For Jimmy, he told himself. "My mother sent you some stuff she thought you might need," he said when Mrs. Osaki released him. "I'll bring it in."

Tears spilled down her cheeks when she saw the box of groceries, and she dabbed at her eyes with a handkerchief. "Your mother I have not met, but she is true friend," Mrs. Osaki said, her voice trembling. "Bread man come no more, and milkman, he take empty bottle but leave nothing. I walk all the way to store, but they not take my money. Money! I must pay—"

"No money," Foster said quickly. "My mother sent this as a gift. A present." At least he thought she had. "If you make a list, she can get you what you need on Saturday and I'll bring it over in my wagon next week. You can pay for that, but this is a gift."

"I get money now and I tell you what to bring next time," Mrs. Osaki said, motioning him to a chair.

She couldn't write English, Foster realized, and he called after her, "Bring me paper and pencil, 'cause if I don't write down what you say, I might forget something."

When he was about to leave, the little woman touched his arm and said, "One thing more I ask. You mail these? Postman not take them when he come here."

"Sure," Foster said, and Mrs. Osaki handed him three letters to Jimmy. The addresses looked like they were drawn rather than written. It reminded Foster of the way Ricky used to copy the messages he dictated before he learned to print.

Foster stopped at the mailbox just inside the city limits, but he didn't drop the letters in until he'd made a mental note of the address. He knew he wouldn't write—the memory of that shrugging "maybe" was too strong for that—but knowing where Jimmy lived now made it seem less like he had simply disappeared.

At dinner that evening, Foster was lost in thought, wondering what on earth he would say about the work of the YWE, when a voice broke into his consciousness.

"*Foster!*"

"Yessir! May I have some more applesauce, please?" he asked, passing his plate. Sometimes he could distract his father that way.

In a calmer voice, Mr. Simmons said, "I asked you what you did at school today."

"I got all my arithmetic problems right, and I threw a pass so far it went over the playground fence."

"That's more like it," Mr. Simmons said, his usual scowl dissolving into an expression of surprised pride. "That's more like it," he repeated.

As they left the table after dinner, Foster's father

turned to him and said, "While we still have a little day-light, get that football of Melvin's and show me what you can do with it."

Anything but that. "Actually, sir, I was wondering if I could talk to you for a few minutes, um, ask your advice. Maybe we could talk in the living room." Foster had seen the curious expression on Evelyn's face, and he didn't want her listening while she dried the dishes for Mom.

"Well, what kind of advice do you need?" Father asked as he sank into his easy chair.

"I thought maybe you could give me some ideas for things kids my age could do for the war effort."

To Foster's relief, his father didn't laugh. "Let's see, now," Mr. Simmons said thoughtfully. "You could save your dimes and buy defense stamps. Get enough of 'em and you can turn 'em in for a bond. You'll be helping your country pay for all the guns and planes and tanks we're going to need and saving money for the future at the same time."

"Let me write that down. 'Buy—defense—stamps.'"

Father looked impressed. "You could collect scrap metal and rubber, too. I heard on the news that we're going to have to melt down old tires to get the rubber we need."

"I guess we won't be able to get any rubber from the East Indies now," Foster said, picturing the world map again. It was hard for him to imagine trees with sap that would boil down into rubber, but it made as much sense as trees with sap that would boil down into syrup. "Collect—scrap," he wrote. He figured the metal would be melted and used to help make the guns and planes and tanks the defense stamps would pay for.

Suddenly the quiet was broken by the wail of sirens, and Father leaped from his chair shouting, "Air raid! Pull the blackout curtains, Ruby!"

Foster's heart raced. An air raid, not an air raid *drill*. He put his hands over his ears to block the relentless scream of the sirens. Get under a table, he told himself. He knew that was what he was supposed to do, but he didn't seem able to move.

"Turn off that light, you fool! What's the matter with you, anyway?" It was Father, dashing past the living room on his way out, his warden's helmet and armband in one hand and a flashlight in the other.

Jolted into action, Foster ran to turn off the floor lamp by his father's chair and then hurried toward the kitchen. "Aren't we going to get under the table?" he asked, stopping in the doorway. In the glimmer of candlelight, he could see his mother calmly washing a skillet. Ricky stood with his arms wrapped around her waist and his face pressed against her, and a worried-looking Evelyn was drying the silverware.

"There will be plenty of time for that if we hear any

airplanes, Foster," Mom said, "but this is probably an air alert rather than an air raid. No doubt a plane spotter saw something hard to identify, and the authorities are playing it safe," she explained. "Get the cards, and we'll play a game until they sound the all clear signal. There's a flashlight in the drawer."

But unwilling to risk having Father glimpse the darting beam of light, Foster began to feel his way to his room. *This is station WAR, in San Diego, and we're interviewing eleven-year-old Foster Simmons tonight. Tell me, Foster, which is worse, an air raid, or having to show your father what you can—or can't—do with a football?*

An air raid, of course, sir.

Foster couldn't imagine anything worse than an air raid. But making a fool of himself in front of Father would be a lot worse than just an air alert.

The next morning, Foster felt more carefree than he had since Pearl Harbor. Not only was it Saturday—it was the first day of the Christmas holiday, too. The war might spoil Christmas, but nothing could ruin two weeks of vacation from school.

"You're up early," Mrs. Simmons said when Foster came into the kitchen. She pulled something out of her apron pocket and held it up. "Is this what you had in mind?" she asked.

His armband! Foster stared at it, unable to speak. Not only had Mom stitched on the white satin letters he'd so carefully cut out, she'd edged the green felt with a narrow band of white, as well. Almost reverently, he slipped it over his hand and pulled it up his arm, feeling the elastic stretch. "Thanks, Mom," he said at last. "That's swell."

Foster had barely finished breakfast when the doorbell rang. He felt a little awkward when he saw Victor standing on the porch, but he managed to invite him inside.

"Hey, keen!" Victor said, his eyes on the armband.

"Oh, that. It was in my information kit," Foster said, his fingers crossed.

"What else was in there, Foss?"

Foster thought fast. "Oh, pretty much what you'd expect—a whistle, a handbook of ideas, the usual things."

"So, what do you want me to help you with? Mom said I can stay till lunchtime."

That long? "We have to make signs," Foster said. "Posters. See, one of the things we're going to do is get everybody to buy defense stamps, and we need posters to advertise that."

Victor frowned. "Kids don't write letters, so I don't see why they'd want to buy stamps."

"Not *postage* stamps, *defense* stamps. You pay a dime and get a stamp, and you paste it in a booklet, and when the booklet's full, you turn it in and they give you a bond." He and Ricky had watched Mel paste in the stamps he'd bought with earnings from his Saturday job before he went into the service.

Victor's frown grew deeper, so Foster tried again. "The government uses the money to buy guns and things, and then in ten years you get it back—only you get back more money, 'cause they pay you interest."

"How much more?"

"You pay in $18.75 and you get back $25.00."

Victor's face broke into a smile. "Okay! Let's get started on those posters."

By the time Evelyn finally came into the kitchen, her hair still in pin curls, the table was covered with posters. "What's all this?" she asked, paging through them.

"Publicity," said Foster. "Isn't it obvious?"

"Some publicity," Evelyn said scornfully. "You haven't said where to buy the stamps, or when to buy them, or how much they cost, or—"

Foster waved away her objections. "These are just to get the kids interested. They'll wonder when and where and how much, and then we'll put out notices to tell them."

"Yeah," Victor said, "and we can use my dad's type-writer for the notices."

Foster wondered whether Mr. Evans would have allowed that if he were at home instead of drilling recruits at an army base hundreds of miles away.

"Say," Victor said as they finished the last two

posters, "maybe you could come over and play Monopoly tomorrow."

Still not comfortable with the change in the other boy's attitude, Foster said, "I don't know, Vic. My parents sometimes have plans for Sundays." He'd decided that calling somebody "Victor" gave him an unnecessary advantage.

"Monday, then," Vic said. "See you."

CHAPTER
6

"Good morning, boys and girls," Mrs. Jackson said on the first day of school after the holidays. "I hope each of you had a fine Christmas and that one of your new year's resolutions is to do your best work here in class."

Foster scowled. How could he have had a fine Christmas without Mel? Without Jimmy coming over to play with his presents? Without real presents, even? Foster thought of the drawer full of new socks and underwear and of the new school shirts hanging in his closet. Shirts that might fit him in a year or two if he grew a lot. At least he hadn't expected it to be "a fine Christmas." Mom had warned them ahead of time that with war-time shortages sure to come, their gifts would have to be practical ones this year.

Evelyn would have asked for clothes anyway, and the little toys in Ricky's stocking had saved the day for him. Foster sighed. At least Evelyn had given him a book he'd wanted, and Mel had sent him a handsome fountain pen. Foster took it out of his pocket and admired it. When he put it back, he glanced around the room and saw that his classmates were all bent over their notebooks, writing. He'd missed Mrs. Jackson's instructions again, and one of his new year's resolutions had been to pay attention in class.

"Do you need any help getting started, Foster?" the teacher asked.

Shaking his head, he opened his notebook. He'd write a letter to Mel and worry about the assignment later, he decided.

January 5, 1942

Dear Mel,

I'm using the fountain pen you sent me. Thanks for the great present. I guess Mom already wrote and told you that we all liked our gifts a lot.

It was strange without you here. Mom invited two sailors from the naval base to trim the tree and sing carols on Christmas Eve and two more for Christmas dinner. The church got a bunch of names and matched them up with families.

Father made a big fuss when he found out, but Mom told him it was his patriotic duty to be a

good host to boys away from home on the holiday.
He still grumbled, but he was okay when they were
here.

   Write back soon!!!!

                                              Love,
                                              Foster

   Foster read over what he had written, pleased that he
had done his patriotic duty by writing to a serviceman.
But did it count if the letter was also a thank-you note
and the serviceman was your brother? He was sliding
his notebook into his desk when Mrs. Jackson announced, "This is a good time for us to hear what plans
Foster has made for Youth for the War Effort. Come on
up front, Foster."
   Foster was prepared, but he had half hoped she'd forgotten. His heart pounded as he pulled on his green
and white armband and hung his father's whistle
around his neck, and he concentrated on getting to the
front of the room without tripping or stumbling.
   "Well, you've already seen the posters about buying
defense stamps," he said, hoping his self-consciousness
didn't show. "Getting that started is this week's project,
and I'm going to need some helpers." Hands waved in
the air, and savoring his power, Foster said, "I want to
tell you about some of our other activities before I
choose anyone."

By the time he had told about the scrap metal drive and the drive to collect rubber, more hands were waving, and he called on Wilbur, the most insistent of the boys.

"Where do we put the stuff when we bring it in? I want to start collecting right away."

Where *would* they put it? "I'll tell you the details next week," Foster said. "You can start collecting rubber or metal whenever you want, but keep it all at home till a week from Friday."

"I'm gonna get more junk than all the rest of you guys put together," Wilbur bragged.

The room broke into an uproar, and Foster blew a quick blast on his father's air-raid warden whistle to restore order. "We'll keep a record of which class brings in the most scrap," he said, wondering how he could do that, "but between now and Friday, see how much money you can earn for defense stamps."

A dark-haired girl in the front row raised her hand, and when he called on her she said, "If we didn't go to the movies on Saturday, we'd save enough to buy a stamp."

The stunned silence was broken when Pam said, "Jenny's right. And if we put our candy and gum money with it, we could each buy two stamps, or maybe even three."

Foster could hardly contain himself. Now all the

girls in Pam's crowd—and all the ones who wished they were—would be sure to buy stamps on Friday. And the boys wouldn't want to be shown up, so maybe—

Mrs. Jackson's hand on his shoulder interrupted Foster's thoughts. "Thank you, Foster," she said. "Boys and girls, I'm proud of you. It's going to take all of us working together and making sacrifices, not just our men in uniform, if America is going to win this war."

If? Foster was stunned. He had taken for granted that America and its allies would win. But what if they didn't? How would he ever learn to speak German? Or to read Japanese? Would he have to march along using that strange, straight-legged step he'd seen on the newsreels? Or eat with chopsticks? Or—

"Foster?"

"Huh?" Foster blinked. The room was empty except for Mrs. Jackson, who was putting a new spelling list on the board, and Jenny, standing hesitantly beside him.

"I just wanted to say that I'd be glad to help you with the stamps. If you need any help." She blushed and hurried out to recess.

"Hey, Jenny," he called. "Hey, Jenny—wait up!"

CHAPTER
7

That clock must have stopped, Foster thought as he stared at its moon-like face on Friday morning. The hands hadn't moved the whole time he'd been looking at it. Finally, the long hand jerked forward, and Foster sighed. The watched clock never ticks, he thought. No, the watched clock never tocks. "Ve haf vays to make you tock," he whispered, leering at the clock's face. The hand jumped forward again, and Foster grinned.

At exactly five minutes before ten, he stood up and announced, "It's time for the YWE stamp sellers to leave now, Mrs. Jackson." At her nod, he led the students he'd chosen into the hall where the custodian had set up folding tables and chairs for them. Foster's eyes widened when Jenny began to drape a twisted red, white, and blue crepe paper garland across the front of the tables.

"I hope you don't mind, Foster," she said shyly. "My dad brought this home from his store for us to use."

"It looks good," Foster said. He barely had time to sit down under the hand-lettered sign that said BUY YOUR WAR STAMPS HERE before the fourth graders burst out of the room across the hall and raced to the tables.

"Aw right, you guys," Wilbur bellowed, "I want you to line up at those tables and keep your lines straight. And keep your mouths shut so the YWE volunteers can hear themselves think."

Foster couldn't help but be impressed with how quickly the fourth graders followed Wilbur's orders, and he congratulated himself on appointing the loud, heavyset boy his sergeant at arms. It was the only job he could think of for somebody like Wilbur, somebody who really wanted to help but would have been slow dealing with money or writing down names.

Foster's head was swimming by the time the hour was over and the money they'd collected had been counted. Not enough for a tank or a bomber, but maybe it would buy a couple of machine guns. Foster was wondering how much machine guns cost when Vic yelled across the hall.

"Hey, Wilbur! I don't see your name on any of our lists—how come you didn't buy any defense stamps? Aren't you patriotic?"

Wilbur, who had just come upstairs after shepherding the first graders back to their classroom, glared at Vic and said, "'Course I'm patriotic. Didn't you hear me say I was gonna bring in more scrap than anybody else in the whole school?"

"Yes, but—"

Pam interrupted him. "My father's a banker, and he says financial records are confidential. He says it's a matter of honor not to tell what you've learned about other people's personal affairs."

"Yeah, Vic, aren't you honorable?" Wilbur asked.

Before Vic could answer, Foster said, "Cut it out, you guys—here comes Miss Cook."

"You young people seem to have had a successful sale," she said, "and I see that you already have your coins in rolls!"

"That was Pam's idea," Foster said, hardly believing he was having an ordinary conversation with the principal. "Pam's dad's a banker, and she brought in the paper wrappers for us." That meant he'd had to choose Pam as one of his helpers, but he'd made it a point not to choose any of her friends.

"One person at each table recorded names and amounts, and the other counted the money and put the coins in rolls," Foster added, hoping Miss Cook would leave before he ran out of things to say to her. He liked it better when she stayed in her office.

"Well, bring your coin rolls downstairs and I'll have my secretary take them to the bank for you."

"Wilbur will bring them down," Foster said. He'd

been wondering what he was supposed to do with all that money. . . .

At the end of the day, the principal's secretary brought a large box into the classroom, and Mrs. Jackson beckoned to Foster and said, "I think this is for you."

He peered inside the box and saw a stack of perforated sheets of pinkish-red stamps and what looked like hundreds of pocket-sized booklets to paste them into. How was he going to see that everybody got the stamps they had paid for that morning? And how was he going to come up with ideas for the scrap metal drive next week? Slowly he walked down the aisle to his seat, wishing he'd never made up the YWE.

When school was dismissed, Foster saw Jenny waiting beside the box. "If you want to come over to my house, I could help you," she said. "I live just two blocks down the avenue."

"Swell! Ricky—he's my brother—can tell my mom."

Jenny's mother fixed them lemonade and cookies, and they spread out their materials on the dining room table. Foster had no idea where to begin, but Jenny said, "Why don't you start with the top sheet and read off the first person's name. I'll write the name on a booklet, and you tear off the right number of stamps and stick them inside." When Foster made a face, she quickly said, "Just *put* them inside. The kids will want to stick them down themselves."

They set to work, and it went faster than Foster had thought it would. "You know what?" he said. "So far, these are all fourth graders. We should rubber band these booklets together by class and let the teachers pass them out on Monday."

Slowly, Foster became aware of the smell of onions frying. He ran into the kitchen and asked, "What time is it, Mrs. Harris?"

"A quarter to five," she said, smiling.

"I've got to get home—can I leave this stuff here for now?"

"Sure. You can come over tomorrow morning, if you want to, and we can finish then," Jenny said.

"Thanks!" he called over his shoulder as he left, almost bumping into a tall, well-dressed man. "Sorry, sir," he gasped. He raced along the sidewalk, cut across a vacant lot, and dashed around the corner, but his steps faltered when he saw the car parked in front of his house. Father was already home.

He'd better use Evelyn's trick and go in the back way, Foster decided, hurrying around to the kitchen door. He was barely inside when his mother said, "Wash up at the sink, Foster, and be quick." Raising her voice, she called, "Dinner's on the table, dear."

Foster had just finished drying his hands when his father came into the room and looked at the clock. "You know I like my meals on time, Ruby," he complained as he took his place at the table.

"And they almost always are on time, aren't they, Horace?" Mrs. Simmons set a casserole in front of her husband, between the jello salad ring and the hot rolls. "So how did the sale of defense stamps go, Foster?" she asked as she sat down.

Father looked up and demanded, "What sale? What's this all about?"

"Remember when you said buying defense stamps was a way kids could help the war effort? Well, I organized a sale at school, and six of us sold stamps for over an hour," Foster said proudly.

Father's eyes narrowed. "What's that around your neck?"

Foster's hand moved to his father's whistle. "This? Well, just like you wear a helmet and armband and whistle to show you're an air-raid warden, I wear an armband and whistle to show I'm a Youth for the War Effort leader. I don't have a helmet, though. Or a flashlight, either," he added desperately.

"You knew Foster was a leader in the YWE, didn't you?" Mom asked. "I think some of the other mothers in the neighborhood are a little envious that their sons weren't chosen."

Ricky, who hardly ever said a word at dinner, chimed in, "I got to be captain at recess today 'cause everybody knows Foster's my big brother."

"Come on, Ricky, give Father a chance to ask the blessing," Evelyn said.

"Just a *minute!*" Father roared. The room fell silent, and he continued in a more normal voice. "You still haven't told me about that whistle, young man."

It hadn't worked, Foster thought, his heart beating wildly. They'd all tried their best to distract Father, but this time it hadn't worked. He moistened his lips and said, "The whistle and armband show that I'm a Youth for the War Effort leader, Father. See how it says YWE on the armband? The school principal was impressed that we'd sold so many stamps, and she said—"

"Foster James Simmons! Is that, or is that not, my whistle?"

Foster's throat felt paralyzed, and his lips wouldn't move.

"It *is* my whistle, isn't it?" Father demanded, and his voice rose as he asked, "Didn't I warn you not to fool around with U.S. Government property? Didn't I?"

As Foster stared at him, wondering how a person's face could turn so red, he heard his mother say, "Now Horace, the child was simply trying to—"

But Father ignored her. "You know better than to disobey me! Who do you think you are, anyway?" Struggling for control, he pointed to the kitchen doorway and said, "Go! Go to your room."

Foster left the table, damp with sweat and almost limp with relief that he didn't have to face Father any longer. Safe in his room, he fingered the whistle and thought, After all that carrying on, Father still didn't

69

have his "government property" back. Intending to hang it on the outside knob of his door, Foster lifted the lanyard over his head. "Hey, what's this?" he muttered. He read the row of tiny raised letters on the whistle and his face broke into a grin. Father's U.S. Government property was stamped MADE IN JAPAN.

CHAPTER

8

Foster's eyes roved over the shelves in the shed the next morning, searching for something for the scrap metal drive. "Slap the Jap with scrap," he chanted. "Slap the Jap with scrap. Slap the Jap with scrap. Aha! Slap 'em with *that*." He pounced on a rusty garden trowel, the one he'd forgotten about and left outside right after they had moved to San Diego. He eyed the toy shovel and pail and decided to let Ricky contribute them to the drive.

Foster was thinking about Wilbur's boast that he'd bring in more scrap than all the rest of the class when he heard someone calling him. Vic.

"C'mon, I've got a great idea, Foss. Get your wagon—your mom said you can go if we're back by lunchtime."

"What's up?" Foster asked as they rumbled down the sidewalk in their wagons, each boy with one leg tucked under him and the other pushing his wagon forward.

Foster thought they sounded like a pair of miniature trains as their wheels rolled across the cracks in the sidewalk.

Vic said, "I know a place where we can get a lot of scrap metal for next week. That's why I wanted us to have the wagons. We'll have to pull them from here."

They had run out of sidewalk and had to walk along the sandy shoulder of the road. Few cars passed, and other than birdsongs, the only sound was the annoying squeak of Vic's wagon wheels. Foster was glad Mel had taught him to keep his wheels well oiled.

When they passed the Osaki place, Foster sighed. If only Jimmy would write to him! Had he found a friend—maybe a new best friend—in his aunt's neighborhood? Another Japanese-American boy who liked to collect stamps and play chess?

Foster forced himself to concentrate on the sound of the wagon wheels and the warmth of the day. He was feeling a little better by the time Vic said, "That's it just ahead."

"It" was a tumbledown house with empty window sashes and shutters that hung askew. The porch was rotted out, and strips of the tin roof had blown off and littered the weed-filled yard. With a whoop, Foster dragged a piece of tin to his wagon, but then he stopped and said, "This isn't going to stay on unless we tie it down."

Vic's face fell, and Foster said, "Come on, let's take

some of the smaller stuff now and make a second trip. I can get some rope from our shed." Now that Father worked at the aircraft factory all day Saturday instead of just till noon, there would be plenty of time to put the rope back when they were through with it. If he remembered.

The boys began to load their wagons with some rusted chains they found near the back porch and then with a couple of dented pans, a hubcap, and some unrecognizable objects from a junk heap by the gate. The wagons were piled high when a horn blared and a truck pulled off the road and jolted into the yard.

"Hey, what are you guys doing here?" It was Wilbur, leaning across another passenger to hang out the window and holler at them. As soon as the vehicle bucked to a stop near the porch of the derelict house, Wilbur tumbled out of the cab after a loose-limbed older boy with the same thick eyebrows and a dissatisfied-looking mouth. The driver, a large, ruddy-faced man, emerged from behind the wheel and looked from the loaded wagons to Vic and Foster.

"These friends of yours?" he asked Wilbur.

The boy shrugged. "They're in my class," he said, but he didn't introduce them. "How much longer are you guys planning to be here, anyway?" he asked.

"Um, we were getting ready to haul our scrap home when you came," Foster said.

"*Your* scrap! This here's *my* scrap."

"Is not! We were here first," Vic objected.

There was a noise like stage thunder as Wilbur's brother began tossing the long strips of roofing tin into the truck bed, and then the sound of wood splintering as the man pried off the door hinges with a crowbar.

Wilbur nodded toward the loaded wagons and said, "You can have what you've already got, but the rest is mine. I told you I was gonna have more stuff than anybody else, didn't I?"

"Come on, Vic," Foster urged, "let's go." He didn't care who brought it as long as it ended up at the school scrap drive.

But Vic scowled and said stubbornly, "We were here first."

Wilbur took a step closer to him and said, "The heck you were. I was here before you was even born. This used to be my grandma's place."

Vic's shoulders sagged, and without a word he picked up the handle of his wagon and headed toward the road. "Well, see you on Monday, Wilbur," Foster said as he turned to leave.

The walk home wasn't any fun at all. Vic was in a foul mood, and they kept having to stop and pick up pieces of metal that fell off their wagons. It seemed to take forever just to get to the Osaki place, and that was only halfway home. Vic stopped by Mrs. Osaki's mailbox, and Foster watched him rummage through his scrap until he found a short section of pipe.

"Hey, don't do that," Foster cried when Vic raised the pipe over his head.

"Why not? It's a Jap mailbox, see?" Vic pointed to the neat letters on one side and sounded out the name, "Ha-ru-ko O-sa-ki. This must be where that slant-eyed kid in our class used to live, the one you hung around with before the war." Vic was about to bash the mailbox off its post, but his hand dropped when he saw a car coming down the lane.

A middle-aged man stopped the car beside them and said, "Anything I can do for you boys?"

Foster shook his head. "We've been collecting scrap metal for the drive at our school." As an afterthought, he asked, "You got any?"

"Can't help you there, sonny, but maybe a couple of hardworking fellows like you could help me. How'd you like to come back here next weekend and pick berries? Bring all your friends. My name's Sam Stone, and I'm running the berry farm now—guess you heard how the government don't trust the Japs not to contaminate farm produce."

Foster was shocked. He hadn't heard anything about that, and besides, Mrs. Osaki would never—

"Anyway," the man went on. "the fruit's almost ripe, and I can't find anybody willing to pick it for me. Guess you can't blame folks for not wanting to do stoop labor when they can make good money at the shipyards or the aircraft factory, but if I don't find me some pickers, that fruit's going to rot."

Foster thought of the apricot orchard and the acres and acres of berry patches that surrounded the Osakis' house. Whenever he'd come to play chess, Jimmy's mother had brought the two of them bowls of whatever kind of fruit was ripe. And now she sent a basketful home with him each time he brought her groceries. He couldn't let those berries rot.

"You mean that about all our friends?" Foster asked. "I might be able to get the kids in my class to come out here next Saturday."

The man beamed and said, "Tell 'em I'll pay by the quart plus they can have all the berries they can carry home with 'em." He waved, then turned out of the driveway and headed toward town.

Vic turned to Foster and said, "How come you're gonna work for that Jap-lover?"

"Huh?"

"Nobody else would run a Jap farm." Vic punctuated his remark by swinging his piece of metal pipe at the mailbox, knocking it to the ground, and then pounding it almost beyond recognition. "That's how I feel about Japs—and Jap-lovers," he said as he picked up the bashed mailbox and tossed it on top of the load of scrap in his wagon.

Without a word, Foster turned his back on Vic and started home, walking so fast he was almost running. He heard the clank of metal falling to the road shoulder, heard Vic call, "Hey, you're losing all your stuff!"

But Foster didn't care. He crossed a street and yanked his wagon up the curb onto the sidewalk, ignoring the clang of a hubcap hitting the road. By the time he turned down the alley behind his house and left the half-empty wagon beside the shed, he was out of breath.

"I don't need somebody like Vic for a friend," Foster whispered as he headed for the back door. Jimmy was the one he needed, and that didn't make him a Jap-lover, either, because Jimmy was a Japanese-American, not a Jap. If only—

Mrs. Simmons looked up from the pot of vegetable soup she was stirring when he came into the kitchen. "Someone left a box here for you a little while ago. It's in the hall."

Jenny! Foster clapped the heel of his hand to his forehead. He'd told her he'd be over this morning to finish sorting out the defense stamps.

"I got dibs on those soup cans for the scrap drive," Ricky said, taking his place at the table. "You hear me, Foster? I said I got dibs—"

"You can have them. You can have all the cans, from now on. I don't care."

Ricky's grin showed the spaces where his top front teeth had been. "You don't? Gee, thanks, Foss."

He didn't care about anything, Foster thought, burning his tongue on the soup.

"I think your friend had planned to work on those stamps with you this morning, Foster," Mrs. Simmons said.

Foster noticed how careful his mother was not to mention that his friend was a girl, and he was grateful. The Evil Lynn might try to make something of it, if she knew. And if she knew his *only* friend was a girl, it would be even worse.

As soon as he finished his lunch, Foster said, "Mom, I'm going over to my friend's house and see if, um, if my friend can help me with those stamps now."

Evelyn looked up and asked, "Would your friend by any chance be a girl?"

"Would the friend you study with at the library by any chance be a boy? I wonder what Father—"

Before he could finish, Evelyn turned to her mother and wailed, "Mommmmm, make him stop that!"

Sisters were an awful waste of flesh, Foster thought as he left the table, careful to avoid his mother's eyes.

The whole way to Jenny's house, Foster worried that she'd be cross because he didn't show up in the morning when he was supposed to. What if she refused to help him now? It would take forever to finish the job by himself, and his handwriting was pretty awful, Foster thought, glancing down at the neat printing on the booklets in his box. He had worked himself into a state by the time he arrived at Jenny's house.

Jenny answered Foster's knock, and to his relief, she seemed glad to see him. "Come on in," she said. "You almost missed me, 'cause I was about to go collect scrap metal."

"That's what I did this morning," Foster said, following her into the house. He hoped that would count as an apology.

It took most of the afternoon for them to finish the job, and Foster couldn't help but think that the whole project was a lot more trouble than he'd imagined it would be.

On the way home, Foster caught a glimpse of Vic riding his bike up and down the street, so he cut through the alley and went in the back way. "Mom, I'm home!" he called.

"We're in the living room."

Foster could tell from his mother's voice that something was wrong. Was it more bad news about the war? He hurried to the living room, expecting to find everyone clustered around the radio, listening to the announcer's impersonal voice report on what was happening halfway around the world, hearing what new territory the Japs had taken.

But when he reached the arched doorway to the living room, Foster stopped and stared. Father sat in his easy chair with his right foot propped on the ottoman and an ice bag on his ankle. Mom sat on the arm of the chair, her hand resting on his shoulder, and across from him, Ricky and Evelyn sat on opposite ends of the sofa. The radio was silent.

"What do you know about that mess on the front porch?" Father barked.

"N-nothing. I came in the back way."

Glaring at Foster, Father pointed to the empty space in the middle of the sofa and waited for him to sit down. "Are you telling me that you know nothing about the pile of junk on the front porch? Think hard before you answer me, Foster," he said, "because your brother and sister both swear they had nothing to do with it."

Foster swallowed hard. "I don't know anything about it. Honest."

Father took such a huge breath that Foster thought of the frog that kept puffing itself up until it burst. That was one of Aesop's fables, wasn't it? Boy, it was a good thing Father didn't know he looked like a—

"*Fos*ter!"

"Yessir!"

"Did you hear what I said, boy?"

"You said that Evelyn and Ricky swore they had nothing to do with it."

Father looked up at his wife and said, "What's the

matter with that kid of yours, anyway?" Turning back to Foster he said, "You'd better be listening this time. That junk is scrap metal—hubcaps, an old jack, pots and pans—the sort of thing I understand you're collecting. Do you still claim you know nothing about it?"

Foster moistened his lips and said, "Honest, Father, all the scrap I brought home is still on my wagon, out by the shed." To fill the terrible silence that followed, he asked, "Did you, um, trip over the stuff on your way inside?"

"He *kicked* it," Ricky said in the loudest whisper Foster had ever heard.

The chime of the doorbell broke the silence that followed Ricky's words, and Foster was on his feet in an instant. "I'll get it," he called over his shoulder. Saved by the bell.

"You!" he exclaimed when he saw Vic on the other side of the screen.

"Can I come in for a minute, Foss?"

Foster shook his head. "I'll come out there. What do you want?"

"Look, I'm sorry I made you mad." Vic gestured to the junk strewn on the porch and said, "I brought the stuff that fell off your wagon, but I guess you must of gone in the back way, 'cause I never saw you come home."

"Thanks," Foster said, noticing that some of the scrap Vic had collected was on the porch, too.

Vic shifted his weight and asked, "So can I come in for a while?"

"Um, this isn't a good time," Foster said. When he saw Vic's face cloud over, he added, "You see, my father's pretty mad at me right now." His eyes strayed to the scattered junk.

Following his gaze, Vic said, "Uh-oh. He's mad because of that?"

"It's not your fault," Foster assured him, "but he—Um, he hurt his foot on it when he came home. Listen, I'd better go before he gets any madder."

It wasn't until he was back on the sofa that Foster realized Vic had followed him into the house. "Mr. Simmons," Vic said from the living room doorway, "I came to apologize for leaving that scrap metal on your porch. I should have taken it around back. I'm sorry you hurt your foot. I—I guess I'll carry that stuff around by the shed now." He backed into the hall, and a moment later, Foster heard the screen door slam.

The silence was broken by Father's voice. "So. You were telling the truth."

Evelyn nudged Foster, and he realized his father was waiting for him to say something. "Yessir! I always tell you the truth. We all do. You've taught us how important that is." He was babbling just like Vic did, Foster thought in disgust.

Mom glanced at her watch and said, "Well, folks, I

could get supper on the table a lot faster if I had some helpers."

This was the first time the Evil Lynn had ever been so eager to help out, Foster thought as he followed the others to the kitchen. He got there in time to hear his sister say, "I don't see how you can let Father talk to us like that, Mom. Poor Ricky was so scared, I was afraid he'd wet his pants."

Mrs. Simmons hushed Ricky's loud protests and asked, "What would you suggest I do about it, Evelyn?"

"I don't know, but I'll tell you one thing—I wouldn't stay with a man who treated my children the way he treats us."

"I married your father 'for better or for worse,' Evelyn. It used to be better, and I'm counting on it being better again. Counting on it and praying for it. So until you can suggest another approach, I guess I'll just have to 'let' him talk to you that way."

Foster was dismayed to see the glint of tears in his mother's eyes. How dare Evelyn talk to Mom like that! Couldn't she see how Mom was always running interference, always trying to smooth things over so Father wouldn't get mad?

"Are you crying, Mom?" Ricky asked, hurrying to her side. "You aren't crying, are you?"

"Of course not, Ricky," his mother said. "Now go ask your father if he'd like me to bring him his supper on a tray, and Foster, you can set the table while your sister pours the milk." She opened the oven, and Foster breathed in the earthy aroma of baked beans.

"Didn't you hear me, Foster?"

The sharpness of his mother's voice sent Foster to the cupboard for plates. *He* wasn't the one she should be cross with. *He* wasn't the one who had hurt her feelings. How come she snapped at him?

All eyes turned to Ricky when he ran into the room, grinning. "He wants a tray! He says he wants a tray!"

It suddenly seemed brighter in the kitchen, and Foster felt his spirits rise. He watched his mother put a place mat on her tray and then set it carefully. After she filled a small teapot with boiling water, Mom said cheerfully, "I'll carry his supper in to him, and then we'll eat."

They had just taken their places at the table when Father called, "Don't forget to say grace!"

After the briefest hesitation Mrs. Simmons said, "Let's all bow our heads, and we'll each say one thing we're thankful for. I'll go first—I'm thankful for my family."

"Am I next? Am I?" Ricky asked. "I'm thankful for baked beans and apple pie."

"I'm thankful for friends," Evelyn said.

Friends, Foster thought. This afternoon he thought Vic wasn't his friend anymore, but then—

"Foster?" It was his mother's voice.

"I'm thankful that Vic showed up when he did, and that he came in and said what he did."

There was a chorus of "amens," and they began to eat.

CHAPTER
9

On Wednesday, Foster was called to the principal's office. His mouth felt dry, and he racked his brain trying to figure out what he could have done wrong. By the time he paused outside the open office door, he felt a little light-headed. All he could think of was what Father said at the beginning of every school year: Remember, if any of you get in trouble at school, you'll be in a lot worse trouble with me when you come home.

The school secretary looked up and said, "Miss Cook is in her office, Foster."

"I—I thought this was her office."

The woman smiled. "It's easy to see you aren't one of her regular 'visitors,'" she said, and pointing to an inner office, she added, "Go right on in, dear."

Would she have called him "dear" if he'd done something wrong? Foster forced his feet to carry him toward the door.

Miss Cook looked up and said, "Foster. Come in and have a seat."

He perched on the edge of the chair by her desk and watched while she took off her glasses and leaned toward him.

"You did a fine job with the defense stamp sale last week and with organizing for the scrap metal drive coming up on Friday, young man," she said, "and I don't want you to think that what I'm about to say reflects in any way on the good work you've done for the YWE." Miss Cook smiled as though they shared a secret, and then she went on. "But because this work for the war effort will be a continuing project, I've taken the liberty of assigning it to some of the mothers in the new School Defense Aid organization, and it will be their responsibility for the duration."

Relief flooded over Foster. That meant he didn't have to be in charge anymore! He wouldn't have to spend hours and hours tearing along the perforations between the stamps, wouldn't have to figure out what to do with all the scrap and rubber the kids brought, wouldn't have to—

"Foster! Are you all right?" Miss Cook asked sharply.

"I'm fine!" he said, leaping to his feet. "Can I go now?"

The principal frowned and said, "'*May* I go now.' And yes, you may. But I'll expect you and your assistants to help the mothers in any way you can."

"Yes, ma'am," Foster said, backing toward the door. In the hall, he stooped to drink from the primary children's low fountain before he went upstairs. He hoped this would be one of the nights Father asked what he'd done at school.

I was called to the principal's office, Father.

Well, you're going to learn your lesson, because whatever punishment she gave you, I'll give you double, young man!

She wanted to congratulate me on the work I'd done for the YWE, Father.

He had learned his lesson, though, Foster thought as he walked back to his classroom. He would never again make up anything like the YWE—not as long as he lived.

"Look, Foss, a nurse is going up to our house," Ricky said when the two boys turned onto their street on the way home from school that afternoon. "Hey, she went inside and didn't even knock!"

Foster broke into a run. "That's *Mom*, you dope!"

Puffing along behind him, Ricky said, "But Mom isn't a nurse, Foss, so—"

The boys burst through the screen door, and Foster called, "Mom? Mom, where are you?"

"In the bedroom, changing out of my uniform, dear. You'll find cookies in the jar."

Foster gave his brother a triumphant look and said, "Didn't I tell you it was Mom?"

When Mrs. Simmons came into the kitchen a few minutes later, Foster saw that her cheeks were slightly flushed and her eyes shone. "I might not always be here when you boys get home after school," she said, "but I know I can depend on you to look out for yourselves. Foster, I'm making you responsible for your brother."

"But I want *you* to be responsible for me," Ricky said. "How come you might not be here?"

Mrs. Simmons pulled out a chair and joined the boys at the table. "I've volunteered for the Red Cross Nurses' Aide Corps, Ricky, and I'll be helping out at the hospital." Turning to Foster, she said, "You might be interested in the Junior Red Cross, dear. If you think you'd like to join, I can bring home some information."

"I'll probably be too busy looking out for Ricky, but thanks, anyway." Foster didn't much like groups.

"Couldn't we both be red crosses, Foss? I want to be a red cross," Ricky said. "Can I, Mom? Can I?"

"Calm down, Ricky," Mrs. Simmons said sharply. "Right now you can do your part for the war effort by behaving yourself and doing whatever Foster tells you to."

Pretending to be a newsboy, Foster called out, "Extra! Extra! Local boy drowns after older brother says 'Go jump in the lake.' Extra! Extra! Read all about it!" But when he saw the uncertain look on Ricky's face, Foster grinned and said, "Come on, Rick—you know very well the worst thing I'm going to say is 'shut up.'"

That evening Foster and Ricky lay on the floor drawing pictures of bombers while their parents listened to the news and Evelyn shaded in the world map she was making to go with her current events report. The word "air raid" caught Foster's attention, and he listened long enough to make sure the announcer was talking about the drill scheduled for eight-thirty. Father was ready for it, Foster thought, noticing the warden's helmet and flashlight beside the easy chair.

The ad for defense bonds began, and Mrs. Simmons glanced at her watch. She turned off the radio and said, "You'll be proud to know that beginning tomorrow, I'll be a volunteer worker for the war effort, too, Horace."

"You! What can *you* do?" Father's expression was a mixture of surprise and disbelief.

Mrs. Simmons flushed, but her voice was calm when she said, "With so many doctors and nurses going into the military, the hospital is shorthanded, so I've signed on with the Red Cross as a nurse's aide." Before her husband could respond, the blare of sirens signaled the start of the air-raid drill, and she said, "We can talk about this later, Horace."

"You can be sure we will," Father said as he jammed his helmet on his head and grabbed his flashlight.

Ricky jumped up and turned off the floor lamp, but no one said a word until they heard the front door shut. Then Evelyn's voice came through the darkness. "Do you think he'll let you do it, Mom?"

"I don't see how any patriotic American could object

to his wife working for the war effort, Evelyn," Mrs. Simmons said. "But I'll need each of you to do your part to help keep the household running smoothly."

That was probably what Father was worried about, Foster thought. He wanted to make sure his meals would be on time.

"What will I have to do?" Evelyn asked, her tone guarded.

"I might ask you to do some of the ironing and to help get dinner on the table on days I'm late. You can think of it as your contribution to the war effort," she added when Evelyn gave an exaggerated sigh.

Foster remembered what the president had said about every single American being a partner in the war effort. Looking after Ricky would count as part of *his* contribution, he thought as he felt his way to the kitchen behind the others.

This is station WAR in San Diego, and we're interviewing young Foster Simmons again tonight. Tell me, Foster, what are you doing for the war effort?

Collecting scrap, sir, and looking after my little brother.

I see. And which do you enjoy more?

Well, you can get rid of the scrap after a while, sir.

CHAPTER

10

Foster was standing at the sink trying to scrub berry stains off his hands when his mother came into the kitchen and saw three heaping baskets of fruit on the counter. "Well, you and your friends must have had a busy morning at the berry farm," she said. "Did you have a good time?"

"It was fun at first," Foster said, "but after a while it was just plain hard work. Wilbur picked more berries than anybody, just like he said he would, but Jenny and I picked the most of all the kids who worked in pairs." Foster still felt a glow of pleasure that Jenny had chosen him to be her partner.

"Well, we'll have some of your bonus berries with milk as a treat tonight, and I'll use the rest to top a shortcake for Sunday dinner. That will give us two desserts that use almost no sugar," Mom said as she put the berries in the Frigidaire. "Did you see Mrs. Osaki?"

Foster shook his head. He probably wouldn't see her again, either, since Sam Stone was going to do her shopping from now on. Foster sighed, knowing he would miss those weekly trips with his wagonload of groceries. Mrs. Osaki had been his last link to Jimmy, and now—

Suddenly he was aware of his mother's voice. "—must feel strange to go to the berry gardens and not see either Jimmy or his mother."

He nodded. It didn't even seem like the Osaki place anymore, with the new sign that had UNCLE SAM'S FRUITS AND BERRIES printed in huge green block letters surrounded by painted strawberries and apricots. There was a new mailbox, too—a wooden one to replace the one Vic had battered and taken for scrap.

But Foster didn't want to think about that day. He dried his hands and then ran through the house to the front porch to see if the mail had come. His face lit up at the sight of a letter from Mel—a letter addressed to him. He slipped the envelope into his pocket before he put the electric bill and a copy of *Life* on the small table next to his father's easy chair. Then he raced down the hall to his room.

He climbed onto his bunk and tore open the envelope. When he unfolded the letter, a photograph slid out, and he gazed at it for a long time before he began to read.

Hey, Kid—

Here's a picture of me standing by the B-26 we took up the other day. Boy, I envy our pilot the chance to control all that horsepower! Guess I ought to be satisfied just to be part of the crew and have a chance to be up there in the wild blue yonder. Let me tell you, it's pretty exciting.

Foster looked at the snapshot again, staring at the huge propeller that was just about all of the plane he could see, then shifting his attention to his brother. How handsome Mel looked in his uniform, and how proud. At last, Foster slipped the photo under his pillow and read on to the end of the letter.

Keep on writing to me so I'll know how things really are at home. Mom's letters are always cheerful and full of good news, but I want to hear the interesting stuff—like what the Evil Lynn is up to, and the latest atrocity committed by the Old Man.

Your big brother,
Mel

Foster climbed down the bunk ladder and took his notebook from the bottom of the neat stack of schoolbooks on the desk that had been Mel's, but now was his. He grabbed a pencil from the top drawer, and back on his bunk, he shoved his pillow into the corner so he could lean back and prop the notebook against his knees. He wondered if refusing to read letters from your son in the service counted as an atrocity, but he quickly decided Mel didn't need to hear that. Mel already knew Father still hadn't forgiven him for leaving school to join the army—that had been plain enough when he was home on leave.

> *Dear Mel,*
>
> *Thanks for the snapshot. I'll bet when you were my age you never dreamed you'd ever fly in a B-26. (Actually, they didn't even have them when you were my age.) Do you think you'll ever fly in one of the planes Father helped build?*

Foster chewed on his pencil and wondered what to say next. Something about Evelyn? Mel had asked what she was up to.

> *The Evil Lynn has a boyfriend named Christopher, and Mom lets her go to the library with him after school as long as she's home by dinner time. Well, one day last week she was late, and when Father asked her why, she said she was at the library with her friend Chris, and I guess Father must have thought Chris was short for Christina instead*

of Christopher, because he didn't start in again on how she's too young to have a boyfriend.

Well, Father still puts on his warden's helmet and goes out to terrify the neighborhood. Mr. Green has been sitting in the dark ever since the time Father pounded on his door and carried on when a little sliver of light showed around the black-out curtains Mom made. Mr. Green says it doesn't matter, since all he does in the evening is listen to music, but it makes me feel bad.

School is okay, but I still miss Jimmy. Vic is sort of a friend now, believe it or not, but it isn't the same. I have to watch Ricky after school now that Mom is a Red Cross volunteer.

Foster read over what he had written, then signed his name and went to ask his mother for an envelope and a stamp. As he headed for the mailbox on the corner, he thought longingly of the copy of *Life* the mailman had brought. There it sat, its pages full of war pictures that he couldn't look at until Father was finished with the whole magazine.

Mel had never waited. He would sit in Father's chair and skim through each week's issue the day it came, Foster remembered as the letter thunked into the mailbox. Why should *he* wait? It wouldn't do Father—or the magazine—any harm if he looked at the war pictures now. His mind made up, Foster started home. He'd look at all the photographs and have that magazine back on the table before Father even left the factory.

Somehow, though, Foster didn't feel comfortable sitting in Father's chair, so he headed for the kitchen with the magazine. "Can I have some lemonade, Mom?"

Her hands busy kneading dough, Mrs. Simmons nodded toward the Frigidaire and said, "I just made a fresh pitcherful, but with sugar so scarce now it might not be as sweet as you like it." Her eyes lingered on the magazine, and she frowned but said nothing.

Foster filled a tall glass and brought it to the table where he sipped the tangy drink as he studied the pictures in the magazine. A ship hit by torpedoes from a German U-boat wallowed helplessly as waves broke across its deck . . . men struggled in the water, clinging to floating debris. . . . "Where was the photographer when he took these?" Foster wondered aloud as he stared at an arm that extended above the crest of a wave.

"I can't bring myself to look at those pictures, knowing that it won't be long until Mel goes overseas," Mrs. Simmons said.

Mom's dreading that, but Mel can hardly wait, Foster thought. He turned the page, and with his eyes on the smoking ruins of a German city, he reached for his glass. Oh, no. Oh, *no*! He stared in horror as lemonade soaked the magazine.

With a quick movement, his mother set the glass upright, and a moment later she was wiping up the liquid with a dishrag.

"It's ruined, Mom," Foster whispered after he had peeled the pages off the oilcloth table cover. "What am I going to do?"

Shaking her head, his mother left the room and returned with her purse. She handed him a dime and said, "Take this and go to the newsstand over on the boulevard, and let this be a lesson to you, Foster."

"Thanks, Mom. I'll pay you back," he said quietly.

"This is an advance on your allowance. Now go! And be careful crossing streets."

Foster started off at a trot but had to slow his pace long before he reached the newsstand. "What ya want, kid? Don't have much candy these days," the elderly vendor said.

"*Life* magazine." Foster's eyes darted over the display, and his voice had a note of panic when he said, "You have it, don't you?"

"Sold out. Everybody wants to read about the U-boats along the East Coast and the fighting in the East Indies."

Foster's shoulders sagged. He walked slowly toward home, trying to figure out what to do, but by the time he turned the corner onto his own street he had discarded all his ideas.

"Is something wrong, young man? You look like you have lost your last friend."

Foster raised his head at the sound of his neighbor's voice, and he waved to Mr. Green, who was sitting on a porch chair turning the pages of a magazine. *A magazine!* Hardly daring to hope, Foster walked up the sidewalk to join him. "What's that you're reading, sir?"

The old man shook his head and said, "Not reading, I'm afraid. *Life* is the one magazine I still subscribe to, because I can make some sense of the pictures."

"Mr. Green," Foster said, "if you'll let me borrow that magazine for a few days, I promise I'll read you every article in it when I bring it back."

A gnarled hand passed him the magazine. "Take it, Foster, and one article will be enough. Or two, if you have the time."

"Thanks," Foster called over his shoulder. His heart was light as he started home, but it beat faster when he saw Ricky waiting for him on the porch step. Was Father here already? Now that he rode the bus to work to save wear and tear on his tires, Foster could no longer tell whether Father was home by checking to see if the car was at the curb.

"He's home," Ricky whispered, "and he's mad 'cause he can't find his magazine."

Both boys cringed as their father's voice thundered from the kitchen. "Don't tell me there must be some good reason why it isn't here! This is the day it always comes."

On his way to the kitchen, Foster tore off the corner

of the cover with the address label and stuffed it in his pocket. He stopped in the doorway and said, "Mr. Green just gave me this copy of *Life,* Father—it was delivered to his house."

"There's no excuse for a mistake like that," Father said, reaching for the magazine, and grumbling to himself, he went to change his clothes.

Foster dug into his pocket for the dime his mother had given him, but he didn't notice the scrap of paper that fell to the floor when he pulled out the coin. Mom stooped to pick up the paper, and Foster caught his breath when she held out the bit of magazine cover with Mr. Green's address label.

"'Oh what a tangled web we weave when first we practice to deceive,'" she quoted as she dropped it in the trash.

"Well, I wouldn't have had to deceive him if the newsstand hadn't been out of copies," Foster said defensively.

His mother shook her head. "No, you wouldn't have 'had to' deceive him if you'd waited until he was finished with the magazine before you read it."

"But—"

"You may discover that in the long run it's often simpler to go along with a difficult person, son."

"Who's a difficult person?" Evelyn demanded, coming into the kitchen. "You weren't talking about me, were you?"

Foster stared at the ceiling and recited, "'Ask me no questions and I'll tell you no lies.'"

"You'd better not tell lies, not to anybody," Father said as he took his place at the table. "And that goes for you, too, young lady," he added when he saw Evelyn make a face at her brother.

Evelyn set a platter of fried chicken on the table and said, "You know I wouldn't lie, Father. None of us would."

Foster bowed his head for the blessing, but instead of listening, he thought of what his sister had just said. They didn't exactly lie, but they weren't always honest. *He* certainly wasn't, Foster admitted, his heart beating faster as he remembered the incriminating address label. And Mel had forged Father's signature on the army's permission form since he was barely eighteen when he enlisted, and—

"*Foster!*"

His eyes flew open and Foster turned to Father and asked, "Do you think a person is ever justified in telling a lie? Like if the Japs came here to kill you and asked us where you were and we said we didn't know when we really did?"

His fork halfway to his mouth, Father stared at Foster for what seemed like a long time. "I suppose you could justify lying to save an innocent person," he said at last.

Foster nodded, his conscience clear. He had simply saved an innocent person—himself.

CHAPTER
11

The persistent clanging made Foster cover his ears with his hands, but he knew it would stop soon. He welcomed the air-raid drill as a break in the dreary routine of the school day, but the pinched looks on the faces of most of his classmates told him that they were afraid.

The class filed out into the hall, row by row, and sat down against the wall. Foster watched the girls tuck their skirts modestly around their legs the way the principal had instructed them to, and then he turned his attention to Mrs. Jackson.

"Are you ready, boys and girls?" she asked. When they nodded, she opened her book and began to read as she walked slowly back and forth between the facing rows of students.

Foster was almost sorry when the bell gave the long ring that was the all-clear signal. Beside him, Sally whispered, "I was sure it was a real air raid this time."

The principal's approach kept Foster from replying, but he made a mental note to tell Sally that Mel's last letter had assured him no Japanese bomber could fly to the United States and back without refueling. Frowning, Foster wondered why they had air-raid drills and blackouts if that was true. It didn't make sense, he thought uneasily, for everyone to be so worried about something that couldn't possibly happen, and he wondered if his brother might have been trying to keep him from worrying. Well, it had worked—in his mind, anyway, since his heart still pounded whenever he heard the air-raid signal's menacing wail.

In the classroom again, Mrs. Jackson said, "And now I'd like each of you to get out your social studies textbook."

Foster sighed as he dug the thick book out of his desk. He wished they didn't have to study about South America. He'd much rather learn about the Philippines and other places in the Pacific where the battles were going on. Places with names like Guam and Rangoon and Kuala Lumpur. Places he'd heard about on the radio news. . . .

On the way home from school that afternoon, Foster said, "Listen, Rick, I have to read to Mr. Green, so why don't you see if you can play at Sandy's house for a while?"

"I'll just go along with you," Ricky said cheerfully. "I've never been inside Mr. Green's house."

Great. Just great. "Well, you'll have to be quiet, so you'd better bring along some comics to look at."

A few minutes later, Foster was knocking at their neighbor's door. "I've come to read to you," he said, holding up the magazine when the old man answered his knock.

"Come in, come in," Mr. Green said, leading them into the living room.

Foster had never seen a room with so many books—one wall was entirely covered with shelves filled with books Mr. Green could no longer read. Foster's eyes traveled from the Victrola in the corner to a cabinet filled with record albums to the comfortable chair by the window. He caught his breath when he saw the intricately carved chess pieces on a board inlaid with squares of light and dark wood. "Who do you play chess with?" he asked.

The old man smiled and said, "First I move a black piece, then I move a white one. Sit here, Foster, where the light is good." As Foster opened the magazine, Mr. Green looked down at Ricky, who had flopped onto the floor with his stack of comics. "I see you have come prepared, young man, but if you and your brother visit again, I will have something here for you to do. Somewhere I have put away the tin soldiers my son played with when he was your age."

Foster saw Ricky's eyes light up and was grateful that Mr. Green had made the little boy feel welcome. Maybe they *would* visit again. He turned to the table of contents and asked, "What do you want to hear about first, the Japs advancing in Burma, the Japs landing on the Solomon Islands, or the Japs landing in Borneo?"

Mr. Green leaned back in his chair and said, "Let's start with the Solomon Islands."

An hour later, Foster looked up, his brow furrowed, and said, "They're beating us bad, aren't they?"

"They are winning the battles now, but in the end, we will win the war."

Mr. Green sounded so certain of it that Foster felt reassured. His eyes turned toward the table with the inlaid chessboard, and he said tentatively, "My friend Jimmy had a chess set, but it wasn't a handsome one like that."

"And did your friend Jimmy teach you how to play?"

"We played a lot, before the war."

"Ah. Then Jimmy was the Japanese boy who used to visit after school." The old man hesitated a moment and then said, "Perhaps you would like to try a game now?"

Foster was at the table in an instant. "I don't want you to let me win just because I'm a kid," he said.

"Fair enough, but if you make a poor move, I will point it out and let you correct it so that you will learn and I will have a challenge."

Much later, Ricky exclaimed, "Mom's home—I hear her calling us," and he ran out, scattering the comics he had left on the floor when he decided to watch the chess players.

"I—I didn't realize how long we'd stayed," Foster said. "Can I come back tomorrow to finish the game? And to read you another article?"

"You may come back whenever you wish, Foster. My schedule is not a busy one."

Next time they went to Mr. Green's, he'd leave a note for Mom so she wouldn't worry, Foster decided as he gathered up his brother's comic books.

"Hey, Foss—look!" Ricky called from the living room when Foster came into the house. "Mom bought a flag for our window."

Foster's eyes widened when he saw the small, rectangular banner with a blue star in the center. "It's a service flag," Mrs. Simmons explained, adjusting the red-bordered white flag so it hung straight. "A blue star stands for a family member who's in the armed services."

"That blue star is Mel," Ricky said importantly, "and if Father joined the army, we'd have two blue stars."

Frowning, Foster said, "I saw a flag like that in the window of a house on Jenny's block, but the star on it was gold."

A shadow seemed to pass across his mother's face, and her voice was quiet when she said, "A gold star stands for a serviceman who's been killed. The woman who lived in that house was a Gold Star Mother."

"But Mel's a blue star, right?" said Ricky. "Right, Mom?"

Foster answered for her. "Of course he is, and do you know what that makes you, Ricky? You're a Blue Star Brother."

Ricky laughed, but then he grew serious. He turned to his mother and said, "I'll always be a Blue Star Brother, won't I? Won't I, Mom?"

Mrs. Simmons hugged the little boy and said, "As long as that flag hangs in our window, Ricky, you'll be a Blue Star Brother."

"Here's another idea for how you school kids can raise money for the war effort, Foster," Father said when the family gathered in the living room to listen to the radio that evening.

Foster frowned. With the School Defense Aid mothers running the stamp sales and the scrap metal drive, everyone seemed to have forgotten the YWE, and that was fine with him.

"You could sell some of these," Father went on. He pulled something from his pocket and tossed it to Foster. "Buy 'em wholesale and the kids can peddle 'em outside the grocery stores on Saturdays. I'm willing to bet that no patriotic American would turn you down."

Foster stared at a small wooden disk. It was about the size of a quarter, and the forked blue and yellow ribbons attached at the bottom made it look almost like a medal. But circling the edge were the words CALIFORNIA JAP HUNTING LICENSE, and in the center, OPEN SEASON NO LIMIT. No wonder Mrs. Osaki had always peered fearfully from behind her curtains before she'd let him in!

"So, what do you think, Foster? How many boxes should I order for you kids to sell?" Father prompted.

"Um, I'm not sure Mrs. Jackson would want us selling these."

"What is your teacher, some kind of Jap-lover?"

Mrs. Simmons leaned over and took the badge from Foster. "This isn't patriotism, Horace—it's prejudice, pure and simple, and Foster will have nothing to do with it!" She dropped the wooden disk into her sweater pocket and added, "I think this sort of thing is despicable."

"Then I guess you think the United States government is despicable, too," Father snapped, holding up the front page of the evening paper. The words of the headline seemed to leap off the page: WEST COAST JAPS TO BE RELOCATED.

"The government's going to build 'relocation centers' for them, going to move every single one of those slant-eyes out in the desert where they won't be able to signal Jap ships," Father said with satisfaction. "Fortunately, our leaders don't think protecting American lives and interests is 'despicable.'"

Evelyn frowned and asked, "But how can the government do that? Send them away, I mean. We've been studying the Constitution, and the Bill of Rights protects citizens against 'unreasonable search and seizure,' so—"

"Is something wrong with your ears, Evelyn? The government isn't searching or seizing the Japs' houses—it's just moving 'em out of them," Father said shortly. "Turn that radio on, Ricky. It's time for our program."

Obediently, Ricky turned the dial, and everyone settled back to listen. It wasn't until the studio audience roared with laughter that Foster realized he hadn't been paying any attention to the show. He stole a look at his mother, and her expression told him that she hadn't been listening, either.

CHAPTER
12

Mom! Here he comes, and he looks mad!"

Foster heard the anxious tone in Ricky's voice and leaned over to pull back the curtain of the window beside his bunk. Mrs. Jackson wanted them to say "angry" instead of "mad," but as he watched his father stomp toward the house, Foster knew his brother had used the right word.

Foster dropped from the bunk and peered down the hall in time to see his mother hurry to the front of the house. He heard the note of disapproval in Father's voice as he said, "I hope dinner's ready on time for once. I don't need any more aggravation today."

"I'm sorry things didn't go well at the factory, dear. Why don't you rest a little while before dinner?"

So the Evil Lynn wasn't home yet, Foster thought.

"I'm too wrought up to rest. I'll be ready to eat as soon as I change my clothes."

Before Foster left his room, he slid the tablet with

the unfinished letter to Mel into a desk drawer and remade his bed, pulling the spread taut. Then he glanced around to make sure the room would pass Father's inspection, and he saw Ricky's jacket on the lower bunk. Foster hung it in the closet, wondering how many times Mel had done the same for him.

Father was still slamming dresser drawers when Foster stepped into the hall and headed for the kitchen. "You'd better watch it," he said when his sister slipped in the back door. "Father's mad."

"Sorry, Mom," Evelyn whispered when she saw that everything was already on the table. She and Foster slid into their chairs an instant before Father came into the kitchen. He glanced around as if looking for something he could object to, then grunted and took his place at the table.

"Lord, we thankyouforthisfoodAmen." Father glowered around the table, and his eyes met Foster's. "Well?" he challenged.

Foster looked away. "Nothing," he muttered, wondering if he would ever have the nerve to say, "That's a deep subject, sir," the way Mel always did.

"Another casserole?" Father complained. "What kind of meal is that for a working man?"

"I think you'll find it quite filling, Horace," Mrs. Simmons said calmly.

When Father had spooned some of the casserole

onto each of the plates and passed them around the table, he picked up his fork and poked tentatively at a piece of potato.

"Did something unpleasant happen at work today, Horace?"

"Unpleasant! That's the least of it." Father put down his fork and gripped the edge of the table with both hands as he leaned forward and choked out a single word. "Women!"

Mrs. Simmons frowned. "Women? What about them?"

Father glared across the table at her and said, "They've *hired* them, that's what. Whoever heard of women in a factory?"

The silence that followed his question was broken when Evelyn said timidly, "When we studied the Industrial Revolution last year, I learned that in the nineteenth century, girls my age and even younger worked in the New England textile mills."

"I'm not talking about nineteenth-century textile mills, I'm talking about a twentieth-century aircraft factory!"

Father's eyes were angry, and Evelyn shrank away and stared down at her plate. Foster couldn't help but feel a little sorry for her, even though he didn't understand why she'd never learned to keep her mouth shut.

"And that's not the half of it," Father went on. "You

know what they wear? Pants! What do you think of that, Ruby?"

"I suppose it's a safety measure, since skirts might get caught in the machinery," she mused.

Father continued as if he hadn't heard her. "And this morning there was a woman bus driver on our route. I felt lucky to get to work in one piece. Seems like everywhere I turn, some woman's trying to do a man's job. When is it going to stop?"

"When this war's won and all the men come back, most likely," Mom said, refilling Ricky's milk glass.

But not all the men would be coming back, Foster thought, and suddenly he wasn't hungry anymore.

". . . Foster. Foster? Are you all right, son?"

His mother's voice seemed to be coming from a great distance as Foster struggled out of a dreamless sleep. "Huh? Wha——?" Squinting, he looked up into her anxious face.

"I've never known you to oversleep like this, Foster. Are you coming down with something?"

He shook his head. "Those sirens last night woke me up." He'd lain awake for hours, or at least it seemed like hours, after he finally got Ricky back to bed. "Huh?" he asked again, realizing that his mother was talking to him.

". . . or you'll be late for school," she said over her shoulder as she headed for the door.

Foster dragged himself down the bunk ladder and

along the hall to the bathroom, wondering if in his whole life he would ever again hear the wailing of sirens without thinking of air raids. Without his palms becoming damp and his pulse racing even when he knew very well he was hearing fire engines or an ambulance. Mr. Green agreed with Mel that the West Coast was in no danger of an air attack, and Foster believed that in his head, but he hadn't been able to convince his body.

Back in his room, he made his bunk, pulled on his clothes, and then headed for the kitchen.

"Hey, Foster!" his brother said. "How come you didn't wake up?"

Foster shrugged. He poured milk over his Wheaties and stared into the bowl, wondering if Ricky had forgotten the sirens, forgotten how terrified he'd been the night before. Foster stirred his soggy Wheaties and sighed, thinking of how his mother used to fix scrambled eggs or pancakes for breakfast. But that was before the war. No, it was before Mom started working for the Red Cross almost every day.

"A penny for your thoughts, son," his mother said.

Ashamed that he'd been caught feeling sorry for himself, Foster shook his head and muttered, "I guess I just haven't waked up yet."

"Come on, Foss, it's almost time to go," Ricky urged, and Foster drank the rest of his juice and went to find his library book.

They were halfway to school when Ricky pointed to a notice posted on a telephone pole and asked, "What's that say, Foss?"

INSTRUCTIONS TO ALL PERSONS OF JAPANESE ANCESTRY. The dark border around the paper and its solid black type made the notice look slightly menacing, but even so, Foster was unprepared for its terse message. "It's telling the Japanese they have to get ready to leave here right away, Ricky," he said when he finished reading it. If *he* was shocked, how would Jimmy's mother feel when she found out about this?

Foster tried to imagine being forced to leave home and take only what he could carry with him, being put on a bus and driven to some isolated spot in the desert. What if someday they put up a sign that said INSTRUCTIONS TO ALL PERSONS OF BRITISH ANCESTRY? Maybe he'd say he was French. He could pretend his name was Pierre. But what would be a good last name? How about—

"Come on, Foss! I don't want to be late for school," Ricky pleaded, tugging on his sleeve.

Blinking, Foster said, "Okay, Rick. Let's go." He didn't want to be late, either—the day had gotten off to a bad enough start without that.

CHAPTER
13

Foster pulled a letter out of the mailbox and exclaimed, "Another letter from Mel!" The envelope was addressed to The Simmons Family, so he opened it and, ignoring Ricky's chatter, he began to read: . . . leaving any day now . . . in the dark about where we're going . . . somewhere in the Pacific. . . .

As Foster scanned the rest of the letter, it slowly sank in that Mel would be going overseas without coming home first. Aware now of Ricky tugging at his arm, Foster shook him off and snapped, "Will you cut that out?"

"But I want to know what Mel said!" Ricky wailed.

"He said he's going overseas, that's what, okay?"

Backing away, Ricky said, "Okay, Foss."

Miserable, Foster stared at the letter and wondered when they would see Mel again. How long would there be only letters, an empty chair at the kitchen table, and the neatly made bed in their room to remind him that he had an older brother? It wasn't fair!

Foster slipped the letter into its envelope when Sandy ran across the street hollering, "I can play in the hideout till dinnertime, Rick."

"Change your clothes first, Ricky," Foster said, grabbing his brother before he could start around the house. "It's your patriotic duty to keep your school clothes nice because—"

"I know, I *know*," Ricky said, pulling away from him. "Because all the clothing factories are busy making uniforms for our soldiers instead of stuff for civilians."

Soon we'll all have patriotic patches on our pants, Foster thought as he watched his brother dash inside to change. Sandy headed toward the hideout the two little boys were making in the bushes by the shed, and heavy-hearted, Foster left the envelope by Father's chair and went to his room. He'd start his homework. Maybe that would take his mind off Mel.

But when Mrs. Simmons came home more than an hour later, Foster's paper was covered with drawings of fighter planes and bombers instead of spelling sentences. He hurried to the living room and found his mother reading Mel's letter.

She looked up and said, "I can't believe he wrote instead of calling us to say good-bye."

"Maybe he couldn't get to a phone," Foster suggested. "A lot of guys must have been trying to call home."

The frown left his mother's face and she said, "I'll see if I can get through to him now." She dialed the operator and said, "I want to make a person-to-person call to Melvin Simmons," and she read off the number at the base.

"Are you going to let me talk to him?" Foster asked, hoping he wouldn't be home when Father saw a long-distance call on the phone bill.

"Of course, but only for a minute, because—" Suddenly her tone changed and she spoke into the receiver. "No longer at this number? Thank you, operator."

Foster heard the front door open, and a moment later Evelyn came into the room, her schoolbooks clutched to her chest. "What's wrong, Mom?" she asked in a small voice, and when her mother didn't answer, she turned to Foster and whispered, "Is it Mel?"

Foster was about to explain when Mrs. Simmons burst out, "He's not there. Not at the base. He's on his way overseas and we never had a chance to say goodbye." She buried her face in her hands.

Evelyn knelt beside her and said gently, "You go lie down for a while, Mom. Foster and I will get dinner." Then, her voice crisp and matter-of-fact, she said, "Come on, Foster. You can set the table while I decide what we'll have."

Surprised at the way his sister had taken charge, Foster followed her to the kitchen.

"If I slice this leftover meat, we can have hot roast

beef sandwiches," Evelyn muttered as she peered into the Frigidaire, "and I can do something with these baked potatoes." Raising her voice she said, "Open a couple cans of peas, Foster."

They had dinner nearly ready when their mother came into the kitchen to take over, and the food was on the table by the time Father had changed his clothes after work.

When they were all at the table, Father frowned and said, "I asked a blessing over this food yesterday."

"Not over the peas, Horace, and not over the carrot sticks, either," Mrs. Simmons said evenly as she bowed her head.

For once Foster listened, wondering if his father would actually single out the carrot sticks and peas, but to his disappointment, it was the usual all-purpose blessing.

They had nearly finished eating when Mom said, "Horace, we got a letter from Mel today saying he was about to be sent overseas, and when I called the base to speak to him, they said he'd already gone."

Father didn't answer, but Evelyn said, "I still don't see why he wrote. Why didn't he call us?"

Her mother sighed. "I've been wondering the same thing. It would have meant so much to hear his voice—I just can't understand it."

"He did call," Father said impatiently. "Last Thursday. Collect."

"And you never told me?" Mrs. Simmons sounded incredulous. "What did he say, Horace?"

"You must not have understood, Ruby. He called *collect*."

Mom stared across the table at him. "Are you telling me that you wouldn't accept the call?"

"He's making money now. Why should he expect someone else to be responsible for his expenses?"

Foster's stomach tightened as he looked from one parent to the other, his father flushed and blustery, his mother growing paler by the moment.

"Now, look here, Ruby, I had no way of knowing he was calling to say good-bye."

Mrs. Simmons' voice shook as she said, "Horace, when your son phones, you talk to him no matter *what* he's called to say. And no matter what it costs."

There was complete silence around the table as Mom rose from her place and left the kitchen, and then all eyes turned to Father. With a muffled curse, he threw down his napkin and stormed out of the house.

His voice pitched higher than usual, Ricky said, "I'm going to find Mom."

"Oh, no, you're not!" Foster shoved his chair back against the wall to block his brother's way.

"She wants to be alone for a little while, Ricky," Evelyn said, "and besides, you have to help Foster clear the table while I put the leftovers away."

Leftover leftovers, Foster thought as he picked up his plate.

Twenty minutes later, he was hanging up the dish towel and Evelyn was sweeping the floor when Mrs. Simmons came back to the kitchen. "You young people have done a fine job here, and now we're all going to walk over to the boulevard and treat ourselves to a movie," she announced.

Ricky looked up from the plane he was drawing and asked, "Even me, Mom? I helped clear the table and dried the silverware, so can I come too? Can I?"

"You are such a trial, Ricky!" Evelyn said, emptying the dust pan into the trash. "Mom said we're *all* going, didn't she?"

As the four of them left the house together, Foster realized that this was the first time he could think of that they had gone out in the evening without Father. He was glad Father wasn't along, but it felt strange, just the same.

While Mrs. Simmons was buying the tickets, a convoy of troop-filled army trucks went by. Foster and Ricky ran to the curb, both arms raised as they made the "V for Victory" sign with two fingers on each hand, but the soldiers' eyes were on Evelyn, and they whistled and called, "Hubba! Hubba!" To Foster's surprise, she smiled and waved.

When the last of the trucks had passed and Evelyn

saw her mother's disapproving look, she blushed and said, "All the girls wave to them, Mom. It's the patriotic thing to do."

"Well, I suppose it can't do any harm," Mrs. Simmons said reluctantly, "and it probably does boost their morale."

Foster opened the door to the theater and held it for the others. The newsreel had already started, and as an usher led them down the darkened aisle, Foster wished they'd come a little later. The war pictures in newsreels were ten times worse than the ones in *Life*, and you couldn't turn the page if you didn't want to look at them. Besides, when you looked at a magazine you didn't hear gunfire—or even worse. Foster half wished he were Ricky's age so he could slide down in his seat and press his hands to his ears to escape the piercing whistle of bombs falling, the *ack-ack-ack* of machine-gun fire.

At last the battle sounds were replaced by band music, and when Foster raised his eyes to the screen he saw men waving from the crowded decks of a huge troop transport ship while on the shore women waved to them and wept. Beside him, his mother rummaged in her purse for a handkerchief, and Foster began to wish they hadn't come. . . .

It was late by the time they'd walked home from the show, and the house was dark. Inside, Foster switched on the hall light and squinted in the sudden brightness.

He gave a start when a movement in the darkened living room caught his eye as Father hauled himself from his easy chair.

"Horace! What's wrong?" Mom cried, hurrying toward him.

Straining his ears, Foster heard his father say, "I thought you'd left me, Ruby. I thought you'd taken the children and left me."

"Don't stand there gawking, Foster!" Evelyn hissed.

Reluctantly, he followed his sister as she shepherded Ricky down the hall ahead of her, but not before he heard his mother say, "You know I'd never leave you, Horace."

But Mel had left him, Foster thought bitterly. Mel had left all of them, just so he could get away from Father. And it was because of Father that they hadn't had a chance to say good-bye to Mel. If only it were the other way around. If only Mel could stay home with them and build airplanes while Father went overseas.

Two weeks later, Foster decided to skip the Saturday morning radio programs in favor of a chance to play chess without Ricky breathing over his shoulder. As he knocked on Mr. Green's door, he wondered if Mel had ever wished that *he* wouldn't always tag along.

In the middle of the game, Mr. Green said, "Someone is calling you, Foster."

Foster looked up from the chessboard and listened a moment, then shrugged and said, "It's just Vic. I can see him later."

"Is that a way to treat a friend?" Mr. Green asked gently.

"He's not a real friend—not like Jimmy was. He's just somebody I do things with." Foster thought of the day Vic bashed Jimmy's "Jap mailbox" and then took the blame for leaving the scrap metal on the front porch, and he felt confused all over again.

"Like Jimmy was," Mr. Green repeated thoughtfully. "I wondered if this terrible war had ended your friendship."

"Jimmy was the one who ended it," Foster said, and his words tumbled over each other as he told how his friend had acted the day after the surprise attack, how he hadn't written after his mother sent him to live with her relatives.

"And now he is at one of those camps where the government is sending all the Japanese, no?" Mr. Green made a clucking sound and added, "Such a sad state our world has come to."

Foster nodded. "Jimmy was the best friend I ever had. I—well, I just figured we'd always be friends."

"Perhaps he regrets now that he did not keep in touch with you."

"Well, he knows my address," Foster said shortly.

"What a pity that you do not know his. I imagine he would appreciate a letter—he may need to be reassured that you still wish to continue the friendship."

Foster felt a stir of hope. If he wrote first, maybe Jimmy would write back! "I'd better go now, Mr. Green," Foster said. He needed Jimmy's address, and he knew just how to get it.

After a quick lunch, he set out for the berry farm, and his heart fell when he heard Vic calling to him.

"Where were you this morning, anyway?" the other boy asked when he caught up.

"I wasn't home."

"Yeah, I figured that out. What's the matter with you today?"

Foster shrugged and said, "Listen, I have to go somewhere now, but I might be able to come over tomorrow afternoon."

"Okay. See you then."

It wasn't any of Vic's business where he was this morning or where he was going now, Foster thought. Vic was a fair-weather friend, but Jimmy had been a real one. Foster wondered if Jimmy really did wish he'd kept in touch. Wondered if Jimmy missed him, if he regretted that "maybe" and wished he'd said he would write.

Well, Foster thought, once he got the address of the internment camp from "Uncle Sam," he'd write so

Jimmy would know he still wanted to be friends. "Dear Jimmy," he muttered, composing his letter in his head as he walked, "I got your address from the man who's looking after the berry farm. He and his wife are taking good care of your house and your fruit. Some of us kids are going out there again soon to help him pick. Last time, Wilbur picked more berries than anybody else. I hope they let your father go to that camp with you. Please write back."

No, that sounded like he was begging. "I'll say, 'Write back if you want to be pen pals,'" he decided. But what if Jimmy didn't want to be pen pals? Foster sighed. He figured you couldn't make a person want to be your pen pal any more than you could make somebody want to be your friend.

CHAPTER
14

What do you think's in these boxes, Foster?" Ricky asked as the two boys struggled toward the house carrying the third of the five boxes Father had brought home.

"Whatever it is, it sure is awfully heavy," Foster said. "You think it has something to do with the war?"

"*Everything* has something to do with the war," Foster said, backing up the two steps to the front porch. Hand grenades, or maybe ammunition. He felt a chill. That must be it—since Father was an air-raid warden, he'd been asked to stockpile weapons in case the Japs landed and people had to defend their neighborhoods. The box began to slip and Foster cried, "Look out! It might ex— It might break."

The brothers were wrestling the next box out of the trunk when Evelyn came strolling along the sidewalk with a boy Foster had never seen before. "You kids need some help?" the boy asked. Without waiting for an answer, he hauled out both the remaining boxes and Foster sprinted ahead to hold the door open for him.

"Who's this?" Father demanded, coming into the hall as the boy was lowering the boxes to the floor.

Evelyn was nowhere in sight, so Foster said, "Um, he was walking down the street and offered to help us."

"I'm Brad Hastings, sir," the boy said, offering a hand.

"You new in the neighborhood?" Father asked.

Brad shook his head. "I live across the avenue. Well, nice to meet you, sir."

He had just left when Evelyn came in the back door.

"You should have been here a minute ago," Foster called.

"Yeah," Ricky chimed in, "there was this guy, and he helped us carry in the boxes, and—"

Father said, "He wasn't the kind of 'guy' who would interest your sister. This young man was neatly dressed, and he knew how to speak to his elders."

"His name was Brad something," Foster said, wondering what had become of Chris, the boy his sister met at the library.

Evelyn frowned as though she were thinking. "Maybe it was Brad Hastings. He's the best student in the junior class."

"That's who it was," Ricky said, his voice excited. "He said his name was Brad Hastings."

Father turned to Evelyn and said, "Polite, well dressed, and a good student on top of it all. Why couldn't you have a boyfriend like him instead of one of those good-for-nothings that keep showing up and asking for you?"

Kept showing up, Foster thought. Once Father got through with them, they never showed up a second time, and pretty soon the word got around. They hadn't been good-for-nothings, either.

"Why is everyone standing in the hall?" Mom asked from the kitchen doorway.

Father rubbed his hands together and said, "Come on in here, Ruby, and look at what I got for us." He took his pocketknife and cut the string that tied one of the boxes, then opened the flaps and lifted something out. "What do you think of this?" he asked proudly.

Sugar! Foster felt a rush of relief that it wasn't grenades or bullets after all, and then he heard Evelyn say, "I thought sugar was rationed now."

"It is," Father said, "but I got this from Mr. Black. It should be enough to last you for the duration, Ruby," he added, turning to his wife. "You figure out where to keep it while I change clothes."

"Who's Mr. Black, Mom? And how come he can get sugar when nobody else can?" Ricky asked.

It was Evelyn who answered. "Father means he got it on the black market. Our honorable father—"

"Evelyn!" Mrs. Simmons gave her a warning look

and said, "You must treat your father with respect even when you can't respect what he's done, just—"

"But, Mommmmm!"

"—just as you're loved even when you aren't being very lovable," Mrs. Simmons continued, ignoring the interruption.

That shut up the Evil Lynn, Foster thought with satisfaction. He noticed that his mother had said "treat your father with respect," not "respect your father," and he wondered if she'd chosen those words on purpose or if they had just come out that way.

"So is it really enough to last the duration?" Ricky asked, eyeing the boxes.

Foster couldn't imagine the war lasting long enough that they could use up all that sugar. He was relieved when his mother hugged Ricky and said, "All our soldiers would be old men by the time one family used up that much sugar."

Later, Father left for a Citizen's Association meeting, and the rest of the family gathered in the living room to hear one of the popular comedy shows. "Listen, Mom," Evelyn said, clicking off the radio before it had even warmed up, "we had a big assembly at school last week, and they talked about the black market and hoarding. They told us it was immoral. Buying all that sugar was immoral. How could Father do a thing like that?"

With a frown, Mrs. Simmons silenced Ricky's wail

of complaint at missing the beginning of the program, then turned to Evelyn and said, "It was wrong of your father, but it's understandable. His family was poor, and when he was a boy he had to do without things he wanted—and sometimes things he needed, too. I think rationing reminds him of those hard times in his youth." She hesitated a moment, then added, "He told me he'd promised himself he would never do without again. I'm sure that's why being out of work during the Depression was so terribly hard on him."

Foster thought of the years his family had spent crowded into his grandparents' small farmhouse. He still remembered how his city-raised father had worked until his hands were blistered and still refused to stop. "I'll earn my keep," Father had told his mother-in-law. "I may be out of work, but I'm no charity case. One way or another, I'll support my wife and children." And when Father heard that an aircraft factory was opening in San Diego, he borrowed money for a bus ticket and came here to find work. When he'd earned enough to rent this house and buy their tickets, he sent for them, and—

"I'd just die if any of my friends found out we're hoarding sugar," Evelyn wailed, breaking into Foster's memories.

His eyes on his sister, he asked, "What if I see Brad again and he wants to know what was in the boxes he carried? What should I tell him?"

"Mommmmm! Make Foster quit that!"

Mrs. Simmons shot a warning look in Foster's direction, but all she said was, "Would you turn the radio back on for us, Evelyn?"

As his sister crossed the room, Foster said, "I have an idea where you can put all that sugar, Mom—under Evelyn's bed. That ruffly white thing around the bottom would hide it."

Mrs. Simmons raised her voice so she could be heard above Evelyn's protests. "It won't be for long, Evelyn, only until I can figure out how to get rid of it."

"Get rid of it?" Foster echoed. He'd assumed she'd make desserts and sweeten lemonade with it.

"I don't think any of us would feel right about hoarding black-market sugar while our neighbors go without, but I have to think of something that won't offend your father. Or hurt his feelings." When Evelyn snorted, Mrs. Simmons said, "You have to understand that he thought he was doing something that would please us, that he was providing for us. It's important to him to be able to provide for his family. You see, that's how he shows he cares."

No one answered, and Foster wondered if the others were as surprised as he was to hear that Father cared.

CHAPTER
15

By the time Foster dashed into the kitchen the next evening, everyone but his mother was already at the table, and she was just setting a casserole on a cork hot pad. He avoided his father's eyes as he slid into his place and bowed his head, trying to look devout. It worked, Foster thought with relief when his father began to say grace. Now if only there were some way to distract him so he wouldn't start in about punctuality and ruin the meal for everyone. Maybe—

"*Fos*ter!"

"Yessir!" His eyes flew open and he snapped to attention.

Mr. Simmons glared at him and said, "Looks like your son felt this meal needed some extra blessing, Ruby."

"I know that casseroles aren't your favorite supper, Horace, but putting a meal on the table gets a little harder every week, with so many wartime shortages," Mrs. Simmons said.

Foster noticed that his mother managed to sound regretful without sounding apologetic, and he wondered if that was something he could learn to do. It wasn't until he caught the words "victory garden" that he realized his sister was speaking.

"—support the war effort and have more variety in our diets, too."

They must have had another assembly at the high school, Foster thought.

"The principal said it was our patriotic duty to plant one," Evelyn added.

Father glared across the table at Evelyn and jabbed the air between them with his fork to accent his words. "And just where am I supposed to get the patriotic time to dig this patriotic garden? You can tell your patriotic principal that I work six patriotic days a week at the patriotic aircraft factory and get up an hour early to take the patriotic bus to work so I can save gasoline and rubber and that I don't have the patriotic time to do anything else." He was breathing hard by the time he finished all that.

Foster saw Evelyn's left eye twitch the way it always did when she was nervous, and he was surprised to hear her say, "Brad Hastings said he'd be glad to do all the digging, and if I do the weeding, you won't have to do a thing, Father. You remember Brad, don't you?"

Father's eyebrows drew together in a scowl, and

Foster quickly asked, "Isn't he the one you said is the best student in his class? The polite, well-dressed boy who stopped to help Ricky and me carry in the—"

"Yes! That's the one," Evelyn interrupted. "You remember him now, don't you, Father?"

Father nodded, and his scowl relaxed into a frown. From the other end of the table Mom said, "I think a victory garden would be a fine thing, Evelyn, especially since it wouldn't burden your father with more responsibilities." She turned to Father and added, "I know how proud you are of the lawn, Horace, but we can't eat grass."

Foster watched Father poke at the contents of the casserole dish in front of him and imagined him saying, What is this patriotic stuff, anyway? Foster grinned and supplied his mother's contribution to the imaginary conversation: Stewed lawn clippings, Horace, and I'm afraid they're not very tasty.

On the way home from school the next day, Foster told Jenny that his family was going to have a victory garden.

"We're going to have one, too," Jenny said. "My parents heard about them on the radio and thought it sounded like a good idea. They're even going to let me plant a little one all my own in that sunny place in the side yard."

Foster imagined picking a ripe tomato, warm from the sun, and biting into it. He could almost feel juice spurting out and dripping down his chin. Suddenly aware that Jenny was talking to him, he turned to her and said, "Huh?"

"I was just wondering what you were thinking about."

Sheepishly, he said, "Tomatoes."

"Listen, Foster, if you help me with my victory garden, I'll plant lots of tomatoes, and you can have all you want."

"Keen! I'll go home and change my clothes so we can—"

But Jenny shook her head and said, "Wait till this weekend, so we'll have more time to work on it. I'm busy Saturday, but you could come over Sunday afternoon."

"I'll be there as soon as we're through with Sunday dinner," Foster said. He liked the way Jenny had come right out and asked him to help instead of hinting around like some girls would have.

Foster's eyes widened when he walked into the kitchen on Saturday morning and saw his sister finishing her breakfast. "How come you're up so early?" he asked.

"Because Brad Hastings will be here any minute to start our victory garden," Evelyn said. "Listen, Foster, if you'll keep Ricky out of our hair, I'll treat the two of you to the movies this afternoon."

Foster frowned and said, "I don't know, Evelyn. Maybe it would be better if Ricky hung around the yard with you guys, kind of like a chaperone."

"Come on, Foster. I'll give you money for popcorn, too."

"Does Mom know Brad's coming over?"

"Of course she does! She said it was fine as long as he didn't come in the house when she wasn't here. Look, I'll give you enough to buy ice cream on the way home, but that's my last offer."

Foster held out his hand, and his sister counted out the quarters and dimes. Not bad, especially since he had to amuse Ricky anyway. Foster glanced at the clock and figured he'd have at least an hour to himself before his brother woke up—long enough to write to Mel.

After Foster finished his cereal and juice, he brought his tablet and pen to the kitchen and sat down at his brother's place.

Dear Mel,

We're going to have a victory garden. Evelyn's new boyfriend is coming over to dig it today, and she's paying me to keep Ricky from hanging around.

Tomorrow, I'm helping a friend start a victory garden. We're planting tomatoes. My friend's a girl, but it's not like you think. She's just a regular friend, not a girlfriend. She isn't at all like the Evil Lynn—I guess I just think of her as a person.

A nice person, Foster thought after he read over what he'd written. A restful kind of person to be with. And she liked him, too. Liked him as a person, not the way Pam's crowd liked boys, always watching them, always giggling and whispering about them. Foster read over what he'd written and added,

Do you think that's normal?

He raised his head as Ricky came into the kitchen, rubbing his eyes. "Go get dressed, Rick," he said, and then he bent over his paper again and wrote,

Ricky just got up, so I'm about to begin another Saturday of baby-sitting for the war effort. Not nearly as exciting as being overseas, but I guess you sometimes wish you could get off that easy, right?
Here's some more crossword puzzles to keep your brain working while you're waiting for something to happen. Write soon.

Foster signed the letter, folded in the puzzles he'd cut from the evening papers, and addressed the envelope to the APO box number he'd memorized. He wondered how long it took mail to go from the army post office in San Francisco to wherever Mel was stationed. Foster looked up as Ricky ran into the kitchen, his polo shirt on inside out and backward. "Hey, where do you think you're going?"

"Out to watch Brad and Evelyn make the victory garden."

Foster lunged for the back door just as Ricky's hand touched the knob. "Which would you rather do, watch them dig, or watch the show this afternoon—with popcorn during the movie and ice cream on the way home? Evelyn's treat." He pulled a handful of change out of his pocket to show the younger boy.

Ricky's eyes widened, and Foster warned, "But you have to stay out of the backyard while Brad's here, understand?" He waited until his brother nodded reluctantly before he slid the coins back into his pocket. "Okay, you get whatever kind of cereal you want while I pour your juice." Foster had learned the hard way not to let Ricky pour juice.

"You're going to keep me company, aren't you, Foss?"

"Sure, Rick." Foster glanced out the window and saw that Brad had begun to turn the soil where the victory garden would be and that Evelyn was busily attacking the larger clods with a hoe. His spirits rose a little as he thought about tomorrow, when he and Jenny would begin their victory garden. Tomorrow, when he wouldn't have to watch Ricky.

CHAPTER
16

Making a victory garden hadn't looked half this hard when Brad Hastings was doing it, Foster thought as he leaned on the spade to rest. At the other end of the small plot, Jenny straightened up and said, "Here comes Vic. I wonder what he wants."

"Hey, Foss, come on!" Vic called as he crossed the lawn. "A bunch of us are meeting over at that vacant lot near school to play war."

Foster hesitated, but Jenny put down her spade and said, "We can finish this some other time. I'll go tell my mom where we'll be."

"Girls can't play war," Vic said scornfully.

"Of course we can, you dope! Didn't you ever hear of the Women's Auxiliary Army Corps?"

His eyes on the garden tools, Vic said, "Well, okay, and bring those spades along so we can use them to dig our foxholes."

Soon they were on their way, and Foster was surprised to see Pam approaching the vacant lot from the other direction. She must still be chasing Michael, he thought.

"Are you in the Women's Auxiliary, too?" Jenny called to her.

"I'm with the Red Cross. You can help me set up my canteen."

After a glance at the jug of lemonade and box of graham crackers Pam was carrying, Jenny said, "Thanks, but my place is on the front lines."

"Then I'll be on the front lines until it's time for the canteen to open," Pam said, and Foster saw what he thought was a gleam of triumph in the glance Jenny gave him.

An hour later, Foster was shoveling dirt onto the strip of plywood he'd found and was using to roof the hole he and Vic had dug. As he worked, he basked in the praise of Petey and George, two of the fourth graders who had joined them.

"That's not just a foxhole, that's a bunker," Petey said. "It would take some kind of attack to blow it up."

Foster worked harder, pretending he wasn't listening, and then to his dismay, he heard Ricky's voice. Ricky hollering to him. He straightened up and yelled back, "What the heck are you doing here? You know you're not allowed to cross the avenue by yourself."

"Father sent me to get you, and Jenny's mother said

you were over here, so I came. He said to get you, Foss."

Father had sent for him, and he wasn't where he was supposed to be! Foster tossed the spade aside and called out, "My courier says I'm needed at headquarters, men. I may be gone for some time." Turning to Ricky he barked, "On the double, private!" and the younger boy's blank stare quickly changed to understanding as he ran to catch up.

"Come on! You know how he is," Foster called over his shoulder, but he waited for his brother at the avenue.

At last they were pounding down the sidewalk toward the house, and Foster's heart sank when he saw his father waiting at the curb.

"Look at you!" Mr. Simmons exclaimed. "You can't go anywhere like that."

Before Foster could answer, his mother and sister came out of the house and Father said, "Would you look at your son, Ruby? Dirty, and sweaty, and—"

"Now, Horace, you knew Foster was helping his friend start a victory garden this afternoon," Mrs. Simmons said.

"And we all know how Foster throws himself into his work," Evelyn said, smirking.

"Well, we don't have time to wait for Foster to make himself presentable, so he'll just have to stay home by himself while the rest of us go to the war bond rally,"

Father said. He glared at Foster and added, "Let this be a lesson to you."

Foster watched the car pull away from the curb, saw Ricky's face pressed against the back window, and wondered what lesson he was supposed to be learning. "Just don't throw me in the briar patch," he said aloud. Suddenly he realized that Mr. Green was calling to him, and he trotted over to his neighbor's porch.

"Foster, I thought you might like to have these," Mr. Green said. "They have been packed away in my closet since the end of the last war, the one my son was in."

Foster took the box from the old man and untied the string that bound it shut. He raised the lid and saw several lumpy-looking objects wrapped in yellowed newspaper. Reaching for one of them, he tore off the paper and exclaimed, "A gas mask!" He plunged his hands back into the box and brought out something that felt hard and rounded. "This has got to be a helmet," he said, unwrapping it. When he put it on, he found that it covered most of his face.

"You can adjust the fit, unless the straps inside the crown have rotted."

But Foster was busy unwrapping the knapsack. He hunched it onto his back and pressed the gas mask over his face. His voice muffled, he asked, "How do I look?"

For a moment, Mr. Green's face was sad, but then he smiled and said, "You look like a boy playing soldier."

Unable to stand the smell of mildew that clung to the mask, Foster took it off and asked, "Are you sure your son won't mind if you let me have all this stuff?"

"Very sure. When he left these things with his mother and me, he told us he did not want to be reminded of that terrible war. It was supposed to be 'the war to end all wars.' Did you know that, Foster?"

Foster shook his head. "But I know this one's supposed to make the world safe for democracy."

"So they tell us, Foster. So they tell us."

"Well, thanks for letting me have all this," Foster said. "The kids are having a war game, and I'll be the best equipped of anyone, thanks to you." And thanks to the canteen his brother had brought him in December. "This gives me something to write Mel about, Mr. Green."

"And where is your brother now?"

Frowning, Foster said, "Somewhere in the Pacific, but that's all we know. I think he might have tried to tell us more, 'cause the last letter we got had all these lines cut out of it."

"Ah, yes, by the military censors."

Mr. Green fell silent, and Foster knew they were both thinking that Mel might be in—or maybe on his way to—some important battle zone.

CHAPTER
17

Listen, Ricky, I play with you every day after school when Mom's volunteering at the hospital, but today's Saturday, and she's home, so I don't have to take you along. You can water the victory garden or something." Foster shrugged into the knapsack and slung the gas mask over his shoulder. He was already wearing the helmet, now adjusted for a better fit, and the canteen hung from the cartridge belt around his waist. With his khaki pants and shirt, he looked like a real soldier, Foster thought, admiring the effect in the mirror.

"Aw, come on, Foss!" Ricky pleaded.

"Nope. The war game is for the big kids," Foster said, and with that, he was off.

At the avenue, he decided to stop by for Jenny instead of going straight to the lot, and as he approached her house, he saw her wrestling some large pieces of cardboard down the steps from her porch.

"Look what my dad brought home from his store," she called.

"Wow! We can make tanks or something." Foster was already taking off his paraphernalia and setting it by the steps. "Can you bring out some scissors and crayons and something to fasten these pieces together?" he asked as his mind churned out a plan. "Bring some rope," he called after her.

When she came back, Foster instructed Jenny to cut one of the cardboard sheets into strips five inches wide, and with a jaunty "Yes, sir!" she set to work. Foster began to draw the silhouette of a tank on the cardboard, and when Jenny saw what he was doing, she said, "I'm making tank treads, right?"

"Right, Lieutenant. I'll want you to make parallel lines across both sides of those strips when you finish cutting them out. When you're through, we'll fasten a bunch of strips together to make big loops of tread."

Foster was so busy trying to figure out how he was going to attach those treads that he scarcely noticed when Jenny took a green crayon and a brown one and began to camouflage one of the cardboard tanks.

When two pairs of camouflaged tank silhouettes were finished, Foster and Jenny connected them with ropes and hung them over their shoulders like sandwich boards. Disappointed that he hadn't been able to think of a way to make the treads actually turn, Foster had rigged them to the sides using Tinkertoy rods and pieces that Jenny coaxed from one of the younger neighborhood children.

"What kind of noise does a tank make, anyway?" Jenny asked as they headed toward the vacant lot, "wearing" their tanks.

"Sort of like a truck, only a lot louder," Foster said, thinking back to the newsreels. "Like this."

His demonstration quickly left him red faced and winded, and Jenny said, "If we take turns doing that, maybe we can keep a steady sound going. Let's try."

"Wow, okay!" Foster exclaimed after their experiment had delighted an old man washing his car and a woman cutting flowers in her yard. "Let's save our breath till we get almost to the lot and then surprise the kids."

Pam was the first to hear them. "Enemy tanks! Enemy tanks!" she cried, and Wilbur picked up a clod of dirt and threw it at them.

Foster ducked and yelled, "Hold your fire, you dope—we're American tanks!" and a moment later, everyone was clamoring for a chance to drive one of them. When he stepped out from under the rope straps to relinquish his tank to Wilbur, everyone stared enviously at Foster's gear. Pretending not to notice, Foster handed Wilbur the gas mask and said casually, "Here, you might need this." He watched the other boy eagerly clap the mask against his face and wondered how long he'd be able to stand the mildewy odor.

"Wow!" Wilbur exclaimed, his voice muffled by the mask, "I can still smell the gas in this thing!"

"Hey, Foss—look who's coming," Vic called, and when Foster followed his gaze, he saw Sandy and Ricky running toward them. "What's Ricky got on his head, anyway?" Vic asked, and to Foster's dismay, he saw that his brother was peering out from under a colander. What kind of helmet was a colander? Why hadn't he found himself a saucepan, like Vic's little brother was wearing?

"I didn't cross the avenue by myself, Foss," Ricky called. "Sandy and I crossed together."

Wilbur snickered, and Foster thought, Oh, no. Oh, *no*! Was Ricky going to make him the laughingstock of all the kids when everything had been going so well? He couldn't let that happen. Foster pointed at the two little boys and cried, "It's the enemy, men—it's the Japs!"

Making loud, motorlike noises, Wilbur ran toward them with his tank, but the gas mask kept him from seeing a protruding rock, and he tripped over it, sprawling flat.

The fourth graders, Petey and George, had picked up clods of earth and started throwing them at the younger boys, yelling, "Kill the Japs! Kill the dirty slant-eyes!" In an instant, all the boys were pelting the enemy with clods. All of them except Foster and Vic—and Wilbur, who had torn the rope halter from the tank when he fell and was now stumbling toward the boys.

Five-year-old Sandy took one look at the big, awkward boy running toward him, still wearing the gas mask, and he shrieked, "It's a giant insect, Rick!" Ricky, who was using the colander to protect his face now, turned to look and bumbled into Sandy, knocking him to the ground, and then fell down beside him

With a cry of triumph, Wilbur threw himself on the younger boys. "I've got 'em! I've got the dirty, rotten Japs!"

Vic was laughing so hard he seemed to be on the verge of collapse, and Foster was torn between the hilarity of the situation and remorse at what he had started. He was relieved to hear an authoritative voice yell, "Stop! Stop that, right now."

Everyone turned to Pam and she said, "As a representative of the International Red Cross, I insist that these prisoners be treated humanely. Bring them here at once, Sergeant Wilbur."

Reluctantly, Wilbur got to his feet and bellowed, "Prisoners, to the rear, march!" The little boys scurried rather than marched toward Pam, who gave the sheepish-looking clod throwers a disdainful look before she said, "Follow me to the hospital tent, prisoners, and we will tend to your wounds."

Even though he was relieved that Pam had stepped in when things got out of hand, Foster was still angry that Ricky had followed him. He turned to Wilbur and said crisply, "Sergeant, when the prisoners are released from the hospital, I want them confined to that bunker, and I want you posted outside to guard them."

"Aye, aye, sir," Wilbur said, knocking the gas mask crooked with a salute.

That would keep Ricky and Sandy out from under-foot and make them think twice about horning in on the war game again, Foster thought, and it would keep Wilbur from ruining their remaining tank. "Nurse," he called, "when the prisoners' wounds have been tended, call Sergeant Wilbur to escort them to the bunker."

Pam nodded, then called to Wilbur, saying, "Just re-member, Sergeant, if any atrocities are perpetuated on these prisoners, it will be my duty to report you to the Geneva Convention."

Foster grinned and stored that away as something to write about in his next letter to Mel. From reading to Mr. Green, he knew that the Geneva Conventions were treaties. Someone tapped his shoulder and he turned to see Jenny beside him, holding the rope from the dam-aged tank. "Yes, Lieutenant?" he said.

"Do you want me to see if our armored vehicle can be repaired?" Jenny asked. "I believe you have our—um, our mechanical supplies in your knapsack, General."

General! Foster shrugged out of the knapsack and handed it to Jenny. "Do whatever needs to be done—Captain," he said, giving her the promotion he felt she deserved. He turned to the prisoners and noticed that Pam had swathed Sandy's head with bandages and was folding a large square of cloth into a triangle. He watched in amazement as she deftly tied it into a sling. "Hey, how'd you learn to do that?"

"I took a Red Cross home-nursing course with my mom," she said smugly, turning her attention to Ricky.

"My arm's broken, too," he announced. "This one. No, this one, 'cause I'm right-handed." He held out his left arm.

Just then, an anxious voice called, "Sandy? Saaaaandy!" and a woman began picking her way through the vacant lot. "Is that you, Foster? Have you seen my Sandy?"

Before Foster could reply, Sandy stood up and called, "Here I am, Mama!"

"What *hap*pened to you?" his mother cried, hurrying toward him.

"I've been at the hospital," Sandy announced proudly. "See?"

Pam stepped forward and said, "Private Sandy has been well cared for at the Red Cross hospital here in the American camp, Mrs. Evans. As a representative of the International Red Cross, I can assure you that he's received the best of care."

Mrs. Evans pulled Sandy to her and said shakily, "For a minute I thought he was really hurt."

" 'Course I'm not hurt, Mama," Sandy said. He

wriggled out of her grasp. "Now watch how the lady fixes Ricky's arm."

"When our Red Cross worker is finished with Rick, can he walk home with you and Sandy, Mrs. Evans?" Foster asked, giving his brother a warning look.

Ricky's lower lip trembled, but Sandy burst into tears and wailed, "I don't want to go home! I want to stay here!"

"Of course you can stay," his mother said. She caught sight of Vic and called, "You'll bring Sandy home with you later on, won't you, honey?"

Honey? Foster grinned. Mom would never embarrass him like that, he thought.

As soon as Mrs. Evans had gone, Foster said, "All right, men, back to your duties. It's time for you to escort the prisoners to the bunker, Sergeant."

"But we don't want to be prisoners anymore," Sandy whined.

Wilbur saved Foster the trouble of replying. "Aw right, you dirty Japs—forward, march to that bunker on the double!"

"You know, we really do need enemies, and not just a couple of little kids, either. Hey, I'm speaking to *you,* Foster," Pam said when he looked behind him to see who she was talking to.

"How was I to know that? You never spoke to me before."

"Before, you always seemed like such a dope."

Foster decided to ignore that. "Maybe we could split into two teams and take turns being the Japs," he said.

But Pam shook her head and said emphatically, "Nobody's going to agree to be Japs, even half the time. Nobody but little kids, and that's no fair to them and no fun for us."

"How 'bout Germans, then?" Jenny suggested, returning Foster's knapsack. "Maybe people wouldn't mind as much being Germans."

Foster swept his hair across his forehead, held two fingers above his upper lip for a mustache, and clicked his heels together. *"Achtung!"* he shouted.

From his place at the entrance to the bunker, Wilbur called, *"Gesundheit!"*

Pam rolled her eyes and said, "I'm going to help Michael and the other guys work on their trench."

After she left, Foster turned to Jenny and asked impulsively, "Did you used to think I was a dope?"

"Of course not! Just because you're not like everybody else doesn't mean you're a dope. I'm *glad* you're not like everybody else. You wouldn't want to be like Wilbur, would you? Or like that Michael?"

That was the most Foster had ever heard Jenny say at one time. "Not like Wilbur, anyway," he said when he realized she was waiting for a response. He wouldn't mind being like Michael, though—tall, good looking, athletic, and smart enough to get B's on his report card with no effort at all.

"Well, I wouldn't want you to be like Michael, either," Jenny said. "My mom says you can never trust somebody so good looking he thinks he's God's gift to women."

A warm feeling crept over Foster and he knew he was blushing. But he didn't care—if Jenny liked him just the way he was, she wouldn't mind if his face turned red.

That evening at dinner, Father barked, "Elbows off the table, Rick," then frowned and asked, "Is that dirt or a bruise there on your arm?"

"A bruise. I got it when I was captured."

"You were captured, were you? Well, I'm glad to see you managed to escape from the Japs—or was it the Germans?"

Why did this have to be the night Father tried to be friendly?

"It was the Americans."

Father put down his fork. "Did you say it was the Americans?"

Foster's heart sank when he heard the cold anger in his father's voice. They were in for it now.

"Answer me, Richard!"

"I said it was the Americans," Ricky whispered.

His eyes on his plate, Foster waited for the question he knew was coming.

"And if it was the Americans who captured you, Richard, *who were you?*"

"Really, Horace, it was just a children's game," Mrs. Simmons said.

"You keep out of this, Ruby. And *you!* Answer my question!"

Foster pressed himself against the back of his chair as his father reached across him to jab a menacing finger at Ricky.

"Me and Sandy were the Japs. Foster said so. We went over to the vacant lot to play and when Foster saw us he yelled, 'It's the enemy, men—it's the Japs!' and they started throwing rocks at us, and this big guy came after us and knocked us down and sat on us and Foster made us stay in the bunker all day with the big guy as a guard, and—"

"That's enough!" Father roared. And then he demanded, "Is what he said true, Foster?"

The controlled fury in his father's voice made the little hairs on Fosters arms stand straight up. "Clods," he whispered.

"Did you say 'clods'? What kind of answer is that?"

Foster moistened his lips and said, "It was clods, Father, not rocks. And nobody knocked them down. They fell."

"But it's true that you made your little brother and his friend play the role of Japs, the role of the most despicable—"

"I just wanted to teach him a lesson!" Foster cried, his fingers crossed under the edge of the table.

Father glared at him from below the fiercest frown Foster had ever seen and repeated, "You wanted to teach him a lesson. Tell me, Foster, exactly what had your brother done to deserve a lesson like that?"

"Well, he knows he's not allowed to cross the avenue by himself," Foster said, his voice shaking. He hated himself for what he was doing, for getting Ricky in trouble with Father to save his own skin.

Father pounded the table with his huge fist. "Richard Simmons, did you cross the avenue by yourself?"

His eyes large and dark with fear, the little boy shook his head, but when his father turned his attention back to Foster, Ricky burst out, "I crossed with Sandy, Father. I crossed the avenue with Sandy!"

Evelyn, who had been silently toying with her food, began to laugh. "He didn't cross by himself, he crossed with Sandy. Did you hear that, Mom?" she gasped. He crossed with Sandy! Doesn't that take the cake?"

Mrs. Simmons smiled, but she was looking at her husband when she said, "He was doing exactly as he'd been told, wasn't he?"

Foster held his breath when Father turned away from Evelyn and locked eyes with his wife. "Well, wasn't he, Horace?" she prompted.

Foster began to breathe again when his father turned

to Ricky and said sternly, "From now on, young man, you see to it that you cross the avenue with someone who's at least as old as your brother. Is that clear?"

Ricky screwed his face into a frown and said, "You mean somebody as old as Foster, right? Not somebody as old as—"

"Of course I mean somebody as old as Foster! You've been crossing with him every day of the school year, haven't you?"

"I just wanted to make sure I understood," the little boy said meekly, making roads in his mashed potatoes with his fork.

Father's fingers tensed around his glass, but before he had a chance to reprimand Ricky for playing with his food, Mom said, "Now tell us about your day, Horace."

"It was all right. Until I came home, anyway."

So was mine, Foster thought. He caught his sister's eye across the table and was sure she was thinking the same thing.

CHAPTER
18

Foster dashed up the sidewalk after school just as Mr. Mason, the mailman, was about to put a letter in the box. Mr. Mason frowned at him. "Didn't know you had a Jap girlfriend, Foster."

"Huh?" Foster reached for the letter and stared at the neat writing on the envelope. "I never even heard of any Jill Ya— Jill Ya-ka-ham-o."

"Well, she's obviously heard of you," the mailman said. "I'm not sure I'd like it if the Japs knew where I lived."

Foster ignored that and sank down on the porch step to read the letter. He had just finished it when his mother came home and asked, "So did you finally hear from Jimmy?"

"It's from a girl in the same relocation center, and she wants to be my pen pal. This is what she wrote: 'I told Jimmy it would be rude not to answer your letter, and he said, You answer it then, so I am.' " Foster looked up, careful not to show his disappointment, and said,

158

"This girl says Mrs. Osaki really misses her gardens. Listen to this part: 'There is nothing green in this place, nothing but rows and rows of barracks and the sun glaring on the sand.' "

Foster looked up again and added, "She says there's nothing to do there, either. I guess that's why she wants to be my pen pal. But the thing is, I don't want to write to this girl Jill—I want to write to Jimmy."

"Write to Jill, Foster. You'll be working for the peace effort if you do." When Mrs. Simmons saw the blank look on her son's face she said, "The Japanese-Americans in those camps aren't our enemies, and when this war's over, we'll all be neighbors again. If we can do anything to let them know that not everyone bears them ill will, we should do it."

The peace effort. Foster liked the idea, and when he said it aloud he liked the way it sounded, too. His mother had been working for the peace effort when she helped serve coffee and doughnuts to the Japanese waiting to be loaded onto buses the day of the evacuation, Foster decided. And not mentioning that to Father was a kind of peace effort, too, he thought, grinning as he followed his mother into the house.

After a quick snack, Foster went to play chess with Mr. Green, glad that Ricky had gone home from school with a friend and wasn't there to tag along. Foster slipped into his place at the table and told the old man about the letter from Jill. "Mom says I should write back to her," he finished.

"Indeed you should," said Mr. Green, making the first move, "and you should write again to Jimmy, also."

"He didn't write me back."

"But he did read your letter?"

Foster nodded. What was Mr. Green getting at?

"Friends cannot always meet halfway, you know. Sometimes one of them must travel farther to keep the friendship alive."

The game forgotten, Foster leaned forward and asked, "You mean that if I keep on writing to him, one of these days Jimmy's going to write back?"

"Is he more likely to write back if you continue to send him letters, or if you stop?" Without giving Foster a chance to answer, Mr. Green went on, "If your friend could not reply because he had broken his hand, you would keep sending him letters, knowing that he would write to you as soon as he was able. Is that not so?"

Foster nodded, and Mr. Green asked, "Do you think a little of your time and the cost of a few stamps is too much to risk in the hope of saving a friendship?"

Foster shook his head, and Mr. Green gestured toward the chessboard. As Foster moved a pawn, he hoped he'd be able to think of enough to say if he wrote to both Jimmy and Jill. She sounded like the kind of girl who would show her letter to Jimmy and insist on reading his.

"Hey, Foss—look how big my tinfoil ball is now," Ricky said, holding up a shiny mass the size of a grapefruit.

"Quiet!" Father roared. "What are you, anyway, some kind of imbecile? When are you going to learn to keep your fool mouth shut when I'm listening to the radio? Get out of here before I—"

Foster was already hurrying Ricky out of the living room. "You've got to be quiet when the news is on, Rick. You know that."

"Did you see it? Did you see how big my tinfoil ball is?"

Foster pulled the bedroom door shut behind them and said, "Of course I saw it—you shove it in my face a couple times a day. Now leave me alone, because I have some letters to write."

A few minutes later Ricky asked, "Is that a letter to Mel?"

Foster shook his head without looking up. "It's to my pen pal," he said, carefully copying the address onto an envelope.

"It's not a very long letter."

"Well, I didn't have very much to say."

"Then how come—" Ricky stopped short when Foster put his hands over his ears. "Sorry," he muttered.

Foster remembered how awful he'd felt when Mel

had used that strategy on him, but it had been a lot better than being yelled at. He folded Jill's letter and slipped it into the envelope.

It was hard to think of anything to say to a perfect stranger, but this next letter would be different, Foster thought, his spirits rising as he tore another page from his tablet.

Dear Jimmy,

How are you? Do you go to school there at the center? School here is a lot different now. We buy defense stamps and collect scrap metal and rubber and newspapers. Wilbur always brings in the most. It's a lot more crowded because so many people have come here to work in the defense industries. We got so many more new kids the custodian had to bring in tables and folding chairs because there weren't any more desks.

Mel's in the war now, but we don't know where except that he's someplace in the Pacific. The censors cut out anything he writes that might give us a clue. He says that so far it's pretty dull, which makes Mom feel a lot better.

What else could he write about? Mrs. Jackson had told them a friendly letter was like a conversation, so what would he say to Jimmy if he were here now?

Do you have anyone to play chess with? I've been playing with Mr. Green next door. He has a set with carved pieces and a board with squares of light and dark wood.

Tell your mother I said hello, and if your father's there, tell him hello, too.

Maybe this time he'd get an answer, Foster thought as he signed his name.

Mrs. Simmons was humming a little tune as she ladled homemade stew into bowls the next evening.

"It's nice that somebody has something to be happy about," Evelyn said as she slammed the silverware onto the table.

"I'm sorry your father thinks you're too young to go to the junior prom, dear, but it might cheer you up to know that I've found a good use for the sugar that's stored under your bed."

"You mean Father's black-market hoard?"

Foster saw his mother give Evelyn a warning look, and a moment later, he heard Father's footsteps in the hall.

"Well, that's more like it, Ruby," he exclaimed when he saw the steaming stew.

After Father had asked the blessing, Mrs. Simmons said, "When I came out of the post office today I saw a line outside the butcher shop, so I hurried over and stood in it. By the time I got to the counter, all the roasts and ground meat were gone, but some stew beef was left. The butcher said meat's going to be rationed one of these days, just like sugar is.

"When I came out of the store," Mrs. Simmons went on, "I met Reverend Anderson, and he asked me to help organize a canteen for servicemen. It will be in the church basement," she added.

"Don't they have their own drinking water?" asked Ricky.

Evelyn rolled her eyes. "Not that kind of a canteen, dummy. She means a place they can go to dance and have a good time."

Father's eyes narrowed, but before he could say anything Mrs. Simmons said, "Reverend Anderson thinks it's important for the church to provide wholesome entertainment on Friday and Saturday nights so young men will have an alternative to bars and nightclubs. I agreed to help, and—"

"You agreed to help. Don't you have enough to do here at home without—"

"Horace, I'm going to do for the young men at the naval base what I hope some other woman did for Mel and his friends. And Evelyn is going to help me."

Foster saw Evelyn's eyes widen, but before she could say anything, Farther burst out, "No daughter of mine is going to entertain servicemen!"

"She's going to help me serve coffee and homemade cookies, Horace, but if it will set your mind at ease, you're welcome to sign up as one of our chaperones."

Homemade cookies! Mom would use all that sugar to—

"After I work a six-day week, the last thing I need is to sit in some church basement till midnight on the weekends."

It was a good thing Father wasn't going to chaperone the canteen, Foster thought, because if he did, no one would ever come back a second time. Not even for Mom's cookies.

CHAPTER

19

Mud balls," Foster said when everyone met at the vacant lot the next Saturday. "Mud balls instead of clods. That way we'll know when a person's been hit, and nobody can cheat."

"What makes you so sure I was gonna cheat?" Wilbur demanded.

Ignoring him, Pam said, "And we won't decide who's going to be the enemy till it's time to start the battle, 'cause that way people can't stay home on the days they have to be the Germans."

"So how do we decide? And what if somebody gets stuck being the enemy two or three times straight?" challenged Jenny.

"Okay, this is how we'll do it," said Michael. "We'll choose permanent teams and flip a coin to see who has to be the Germans today, and whichever side loses the battle has to be the Germans next time. That way everybody fights their hardest."

Foster was about to object, since he was always the last one picked for a team, but to his surprise, he heard Michael say, "Foster and I will be the captains, okay?"

"Okay," Vic said, "but what about the girls? I'm not going to get in trouble for throwing mud balls at girls."

"We'll work behind the lines, making sure you guys don't run out of ammunition," Jenny said, "and I'll be on Foster's team."

"Fine," said Pam. "I wanted to be on Michael's side anyway. And Michael gets to choose first."

Michael immediately chose Wilbur, Foster chose Vic, and then the captains chose Petey, George, and the other third and fourth graders. After everyone had been picked, Jenny said, "Since Michael chose first, Foster gets first pick of the defenses."

Foster hated to give up the bunker he and Vic had made, but he knew the long trench Michael and Wilbur had finished that morning would give his side the best chance of winning. "We'll take the trench," he announced, and fishing in his pocket, he pulled out a nickel. "My coin, your call."

"Heads," Michael said tersely. Everyone gathered around, and Foster could feel the tension mount. He flipped the coin and watched it arc upward, then spin its way down.

"Tails," Michael said, his disappointment evident.

Above the chorus of groans and cheers, Foster said, "Then you guys are the Germans."

"For today, but after that, we'll be the Americans, 'cause we're gonna beat the— We're gonna beat the heck out of you."

As the disgruntled enemies melted away, Jenny said brightly, "Who'd have thought Michael would be such a sour loser!"

"Okay, Americans," Foster said, "get back here as soon after lunch as you can, and everybody bring a bucket of water so we can make our mud balls. I'll explain our strategy while we work."

"Aren't you coming?" Vic asked when Foster hunkered down in the trench.

He shook his head and said, "Somebody has to stay here to prevent sabotage—look over there."

The others turned just in time to see Wilbur duck around the corner of the school, and Jenny said, "I'll bring you back a sandwich, then."

After the others left, Foster pulled out the folding shovel he'd found in the knapsack and used it to loosen the parched dirt in the bottom of the trench. After he scooped some of it aside, leaving a small, bowl-like depression, he poured in the water from his canteen and stirred with the shovel. Working quickly, he added more dirt, stirring until his mixture seemed to be the right consistency, and then he molded three good-sized mud balls.

There. Firm enough to stick together but soft enough to be messy when they hit. With a mud ball in each hand and another in easy reach, Foster waited, his breathing shallow, his ears straining to hear the scuff of feet in the dry grass.

But to his surprise, instead of footsteps, Foster heard "NYEEEEEAYRRrrrrrummm!" His body tense, he whispered, "Enemy aircraft at two o'clock. Come on, men, let's take it out." As the sound grew closer, Foster raised his head enough to peer over the dirt piled in front of the trench. There was Wilbur, running heavily across the lot, arms outstretched, banking and circling as he came.

He'd just assumed Wilbur would be running straight toward him. His only hope was to startle his attacker, so Foster rose to his feet and yelled, "Ack-ack-ack-ack-ack-ack-ACK!"

Just as he'd hoped, his machine-gun fire brought Wilbur to a halt, and Foster stared right at the middle button on the other boy's shirt as he hurled a mud ball. It hit, splattering mud all across Wilbur's chest.

"Hey!" the boy bellowed. "Look what you done!"

Foster had no time to savor his success, because Wilbur was charging straight for him. "You're dead, you dope!" he hollered, throwing his second mud ball. To his dismay, it missed by a yard.

"*You're* gonna be dead when I get my hands on—

oof!" Wilbur tripped over a shovel hidden by the dry weeds and went sprawling.

With the last mud ball in his hand, Foster climbed out of the trench and ran toward Wilbur, yelling, "Admit you're dead or I'll mash this in your face!" He rolled the fat boy onto his back and stood over him with the dripping mud ball in his hand.

But Wilbur ignored the threat. "Ohhhh," he moaned, "I think I really am dead, and if I'm not, my mom's gonna kill me for what you done to my shirt."

"Death is the penalty for sabotage in wartime," Foster said, pretty sure that was true. "But right now, you're a prisoner of war and I'm taking you to the stockade. That's over in the shade by the Red Cross hospital," he added. Americans were humane—they wouldn't keep their prisoners in the hot sun. "Say, you really scraped your hands when you fell," Foster said. He wiped his own muddy hands on his pants and handed Wilbur one of Pam's white cloth squares, saying, "Here, clean yourself off."

This is station WAR in San Diego, and we have a report just in from the battlefield: General Simmons today aided a wounded Nazi saboteur after single-handedly thwarting the German's attempt to—

"Hey, Foster!" Jenny called as she hurried toward them, her left arm outstretched to counterbalance the bucket of water she was carrying. "I've got your lunch."

Foster felt Wilbur's eyes on him as he unwrapped the sandwich, so he handed him half and began to divide up the graham crackers. *Our war correspondent also reports that General Simmons later shared his meager rations with a prisoner of war in a camp near—*

"Hey, Foss! Sandy's mother said we could play."

To his dismay, Foster saw Ricky and Sandy running toward him, with Vic slouching along some distance behind them.

"You two can be our guards," Foster said, quickly thinking of a way to keep them occupied. "Wilbur's a prisoner of war."

Ricky frowned and asked, "We aren't Japs this time, are we?"

And Sandy said, "I don't think we can stop him if he tries to get away."

"You two are our British allies, and this prison's much too strong for anybody to get away from. Just look at these walls." With a stick, Foster marked off a square around Wilbur, adding, "Those are the walls, and they're ten feet high, okay?"

Jenny said nervously, "Listen, Foster, we'd better start making ammunition, 'cause here comes Michael with his wagon full of water buckets. Didn't you bring back any water, Vic?"

Vic hung his head in embarrassment, but Foster said, "Don't worry about it." Beckoning the others away from

Wilbur, he whispered, "We'll take Michael's. See, he's headed this way, so Jenny and I will distract him while you run over to the bunker, steal a couple of buckets out of his wagon, and empty the water into our trench. Okay, Vic?"

Vic was almost to the trench, a bucket in each hand, when Sandy asked, "What's Victor doing, Foss?"

"Hey, no fair!" cried Michael. "Come on, Wilbur, get over to the bunker and start making mud balls."

"You can't escape from there—those walls have barbed wire all across the top," Foster yelled as Wilbur burst out of prison, followed at a safe distance by his two small guards. His heart racing, Foster said, "Come on, Jenny," and the two of them ran toward the trench, carrying her water bucket between them.

Foster saw at once that Vic's water had soaked into the bottom of the trench, and he instructed, "Dig up that damp soil, Vic, and I'll stir in the rest of our water. Jenny, you keep watch." The boys dug and stirred frantically until Foster said, "It's ready," and they began to scrabble up handfuls of mud.

"Hurry, Foster!" Jenny cried. "They're running right at us!"

That was just what he wanted to hear. The blood pounded in Foster's head as he stood up and took aim. "You're dead, Michael! Gut shot!" he shouted, ducking as Wilbur's mud ball whizzed past.

"Yay! I got Wilbur—he's dead too!" Vic cheered. "We *won!*"

"No fair!" cried Michael. "Not all our men were here."

Foster shrugged. "Not all our men were here, either. Looks like you guys have to be the Germans again next week."

"Hey, did you guys start the war without me?" Pam called.

"It's the Red Cross, with plasma for the German casualties," Foster cried as Pam hurried toward them.

She set down the two half-filled water buckets she'd been lugging and looked from one boy to another. "Honestly!" she said, wrinkling her nose in disgust. "As a representative of the International Red Cross, I'm banning the use of mud balls by both sides. From now on, if you're tagged, you're wounded, and when you've been wounded three times, you're dead."

But Michael said, "Unh, *uh*. We're going to kill them with mud balls, just like they killed us. You can't turn this war into a game of tag after what they've done to us. What *he's* done," he added, pointing at Foster.

"Yeah," Wilbur agreed, "we ain't had our ups."

"If you're worried about getting dirty, you don't have to play, Pam," Jenny said sweetly.

Glaring at her, Pam said, "I just think we ought to have some rules, like not starting the war till everybody's here."

Foster shrugged. "It wouldn't have started early if Wilbur hadn't tried to sabotage our defenses while everybody was gone."

Wilbur stared at Foster. "Man, you're crazy! I wasn't gonna mess up no trench that took me and Michael and the others almost two days to dig. I was minding my own business when you attacked me."

"Then how come you were skulking around behind the school?"

Wilbur scowled and muttered, "Waiting for everybody to leave. I don't eat no lunch."

Foster was about to remind him that he'd just wolfed down half of *his* lunch, but then he remembered how Wilbur hung around the playground at noon on school days when everyone else headed home.

"Exactly what were you doing that made Foster think you were going to destroy his trench, Wilbur?" Pam asked.

"I was being a P-40 Warhawk, and I wasn't nowhere near him!"

Pam turned to Foster and demanded, "Is it true that you attacked him when he was flying his P-40 even though he wasn't threatening you?"

"It wasn't a P-40, it was a Messerschmidt, and it was circling all around like it was going to attack, so I—"

"Planes don't circle around when they attack," Wilbur said scornfully. "Don't you know nothing?"

Foster felt his face grow warm. "I—I guess I forgot.

But enemy planes are fair game even when they aren't attacking."

"I have an idea," Jenny said brightly. "Why don't we have the next battle now instead of waiting a week?"

Foster followed her gaze and saw George approaching, water splashing from the bucket he was carrying. "Yeah, why don't we?" he agreed, realizing that the enemy had no water left.

The "Germans" ran toward their bunker, cheering as Petey hurried up with two small pails. Foster's heart sank when he saw that his side had lost its advantage, but he squared his shoulders and began to instruct his troops. Pointing to the mound of dirt in front of the trench, he said, "Vic, fill those buckets halfway with dirt from our earthworks. George, pour a little water into the bucket while I stir it into mud, and Jenny, you make the ammunition."

"We're going to be a mobile force," Foster explained as they worked. "While the Germans are still stockpiling weapons, we'll dash over there and attack 'em," he said. "Jenny will make more mud balls and put them in the extra buckets, and our British Allies will run the buckets back and forth to us. Got that?"

"We should come at 'em from two sides," Vic said. "Me and him will take the left," he added, pointing to a newcomer, "and Sandy will be our logistic support. You can have George and Ricky."

Foster could almost see the headline: AMERICAN

GENERAL, TOP AIDE CONFER; PLAN BATTLE STRATEGY. He loaded his arms with the mud balls he'd made and whispered, "Okay, let's go."

It was Pam who spotted them first and screeched, "They're attacking us! Somebody *do* something!"

Foster aimed about a foot above Michael's bent figure and let a mud ball fly. "You're dead, Kraut," he yelled as it caught the enemy in the middle of the chest when he leaped to his feet. George's mud ball fell short, but Vic's hit Wilbur in the shoulder as he charged toward Foster.

Foster's next throw was wild, and Wilbur dodged Vic's, but his last mud ball hit right in the center of Wilbur's chest. "Another dead Kraut!" Foster yelled, but Wilbur kept coming. "Hey, you're *dead*, Wilbur!" Foster shouted, and backing away, he stumbled over the bucket of mud balls his brother had abandoned.

Foster screwed his eyes shut when he saw what looked like a muddy walrus looming above him. He steeled himself for the impact and felt a terrible weight on his chest just before something cold and oozy smashed into his face.

He couldn't call for help. He couldn't even breathe. As he writhed under the pressure on his chest and tried to turn his head, Wilbur yelled gleefully, "I've blown the face right off their general—and with his own mud, too!"

And then Foster heard running footsteps, and Jenny cried, "You can't do that, Wilbur, 'cause you're dead!"

"Maybe so, but I died happy," Wilbur said, and Foster felt the pressure on his chest ease, then disappear.

With almost his last breath, a German commando today felled a valiant American general who had just led his combined U.S. and Allied forces on a daring attack. Station WAR joins the American people in a moment of silence in honor of General Foster Sim—

Suddenly Jenny's voice interrupted the broadcast. "Come on, Americans, we can't let them get away with this! George, you coward, get over there and help Vic—and the rest of you better help, too!"

The untried American troops faltered when their leader was struck down, and— When shrieks and yells came from the direction of the bunker, Foster sat up and peered at the enemy, then quickly backtracked to edit his news commentary: *—but his courageous second-in-command saved the day by overrunning the enemy, destroying the entire German force.*

"Are you okay, Foster?" Jenny knelt beside him and began to wipe the mud off his face with one of the Red Cross bandages.

Pam ran up and asked, "Hey, what do you think you're doing?"

Without stopping, Jenny said, "Cleaning the blood off the general's face. What does it look like I'm doing?"

"Well, you can't use Red Cross equipment without permission."

"Well, I don't take orders from Nazis. How's that, Foster?"

His face felt like it had been rubbed with coarse sandpaper, but Foster managed to say, "It's fine, Jenny. Thanks."

Jenny held the muddy cloth out to Pam and said, "Here's your Red Cross equipment, nurse."

Pam drew back in disgust and said, "Our standards of sanitation don't allow the use of contaminated supplies. Kindly dispose of that appropriately," she added as she stalked away.

"Okay, Nazi," Jenny said cheerfully, and to Foster's surprise, she balled up the muddy cloth and threw it after the other girl. "Darn," she said when it fell short.

"You okay, Foster?" Michael called, running up to them.

Foster nodded. "Guess you guys have to be the Germans again next week," he said, trying not to sound smug.

"But that's going to be the last time," Michael said grimly. "Just you wait."

Foster felt a chill. "Well, having a soldier who's immortal does give you kind of an advantage," he said.

"Pam's talking to him now," Michael said. "We don't need an advantage like that to whip you guys. You'll see."

Foster, Vic, and Jenny left the vacant lot a few minutes later, followed by the two little boys. When the muddy group approached Jenny's house, her mother was watering the victory garden. "Goodness, what have you kids been up to?" she cried.

"We just handed the Germans a major defeat," Foster told her.

"Well, I certainly wish someone would do the same for the Japs," she said. "Be sure you put my bucket around back, Jenny."

Oh, no. Oh, *no*! They'd left their buckets at the lot!

Vic dashed off, but Foster had a feeling that it was too late. By now, the Germans probably had commandeered all their buckets. *With their ability to manufacture munitions severely limited, American forces will be at a significant disadvantage in future encounters with the enemy. It remains to be seem whether the resourcefulness of their commanding officer will—*

"Well, if the Germans got our buckets, we'll just show up late next week, run them off with our tanks, and take all the mud balls they've made," Jenny said.

"Yeah, 'cause I'll bet next time they'll make their ammunition in buckets, too," Foster agreed. "Listen, Ricky and I had better get on home. Tell Vic that Sandy's with us, okay?"

By the time Vic showed up, Foster was grimly scraping mud from Sandy's shoes. He had already supervised the little boys as they scrubbed the dirt from their arms and legs at the hose, and he'd used the cleanest part of his own shirt to wash their faces.

"Oh, great," Vic said. "What's Mom going to say when she sees him all wet like that?"

"Well, she's the one who said he could play," Foster answered shortly. "The Germans got all our buckets, didn't they?"

Vic nodded as he turned on the hose and began to wash. "Jenny told me the plan for next week."

Before Foster could reply, the back door opened. Father stood for a moment, hands on his hips, and surveyed the gushing hose and the trampled, muddy grass before he turned to Foster and asked, "Why isn't he doing that over at his own house?"

Foster didn't know what to say, but Vic squished through the sodden grass to the faucet and turned off the water. "Sorry, sir," he said. "I'll leave as soon as I wind up your hose."

"And what do you two have to say for yourselves?" Father demanded after Vic and Sandy headed home.

"We didn't realize how late it was," Foster said lamely.

Father gave the two of them a malevolent look before he turned away, muttering, "It's a fine thing when a man comes home after a hard day's work and nobody's there to greet him."

"Nobody's there? Where's Mom?" Ricky cried as he and Foster followed Father inside.

"She and Evelyn are over at the church setting things up for that canteen of theirs. She left us a note—and a cold supper."

Ricky exclaimed, "And cookies! She baked cookies for the soldiers, and she left some for us." He read the note taped to the counter. "It says 'Cookies in the tin for your dessert.'"

"I wondered if she'd ever get around to using that sugar I bought for her," Father grumbled.

This is station WAR in San Diego, and we've scheduled another interview with Foster Simmons. Tell us, son, is there any truth to the rumor that your mother is hoarding black-market sugar?

None at all, sir. My mother uses just about all the sugar in the house to bake cookies for the canteen at our church.

CHAPTER

20

'll get it," Foster said when the doorbell rang.

But Father pushed his chair away from the table and said, "*I'll* get it." From the kitchen doorway, he glared at Foster and said, "Make sure you're still here when I get back."

Foster nodded, and for the rest of the meal he moved his food around on his plate, grateful that no one tried to say anything to make him feel better. It was his own fault. He shouldn't have taken those floor mats from the back seat of the car without asking if he could have them for the rubber drive.

Beside him, Ricky said, "I'm through, Mom. Can I go see who Father's talking to all this time?"

"Why don't you go outside and water the little plants in the victory garden for me instead, dear?"

"But I want to see who—"

"Honestly, Ricky!" Evelyn said. "Just go outside, okay? Can't you see Mom's trying to keep you from being yelled at? Or have you forgotten how mad Father was when he left to answer the door?"

Foster remembered. He stared down at the blob of mashed potatoes and the uneaten slice of Spam on his plate and wondered if he was going to be in even more trouble for wasting food. He tried to think of the starving children in Europe, but all he could think of was his father's anger, and he swallowed hard.

"Are you going to finish that?"

It was Evelyn's voice, sympathetic for once instead of impatient, and Foster shook his head. The common enemy, that's what Father was, he thought, watching guiltily as Evelyn scraped the rest of his meal into the garbage.

Foster heard the rumble of men's voices and the sound of the front door closing, and he knew that any minute now he would have to face his father. To calm himself, Foster began silently counting backward from one thousand: Nine hundred ninety-nine, nine hundred ninety-eight—

Startled by the snap of a dish towel, Foster looked up.

"Didn't you hear Mom say for you to go see what's keeping Father?" Evelyn asked, and Foster noticed that except for the pots and pans, the dishes were done.

Father must have walked outside with his visitor, because it was awfully quiet in the living room, Foster thought as he started down the hall. He stopped short when he saw Father sitting bolt upright in his easy chair, staring straight ahead. He was alone, and he seemed to be looking right through Foster.

He wasn't dead, was he? Foster's heart raced, but his feet seemed rooted to the floor. As he stood wondering what to do, a tear rolled down his father's cheek and splashed onto his shirt. Foster backed away, then turned and ran to the kitchen, calling, "Mom! Mom!"

They collided in the doorway, and his mother said, "Foster! What on earth—"

"Something's the matter with Father! You've got to do something!"

"Where—"

"In the living room." Foster pressed himself against the wall so she could pass, then turned to his sister and said, "He was crying, Evelyn. Father was crying!"

Evelyn's eyes grew wide, and she brushed by him. Foster watched her hesitate in the living room doorway, then slip inside, her dish towel clutched in one hand. He was still standing in the kitchen wondering what to do when Ricky burst through the back door calling, "Mom! Hey, Mom!"

The little boy stopped short when he saw that the kitchen was empty except for Foster. "Where's Mom?"

Holding a finger to his lips Foster said, "Something's wrong, Rick."

"With *Mom*?"

"With Father," Foster said quickly.

"What's wrong with him?" The hysterical edge was gone from Ricky's voice.

Foster shrugged, and before he could answer, Evelyn called, "Mom wants you to come here."

"Me?" Ricky asked, pointing to himself. "Me? Does she mean me, or you?"

"She means both of us," Foster said, wondering how he could be so certain of that. He pushed his brother into the living room ahead of him and nudged him onto the sofa next to Evelyn. The last time the three of them had been lined up here was the day Father hurt his foot kicking the scrap metal Vic had left on the front porch. It was hard to believe that this blank-faced man was the same person who had frightened them so that day, the same person who had frightened *him* less than half an hour ago.

Ricky whimpered, "What's the matter, Mom?"

Mrs. Simmons sat on the arm of the chair with one hand resting on her husband's shoulder, and her face was wet with tears. Now Foster was filled with foreboding. Mel. "Is Mel— Did something happen to Mel?"

"He's missing in action," Mrs. Simmons said, her voice shaking. "An officer came and told your father."

"Who's missing? Is it Mel? What do they mean, 'missing'?" Ricky's voice was shrill. "What do they mean?"

Through her tears, his mother said, "It's a way of saying they don't know where somebody is, Ricky. They mean nobody has seen Mel since a battle, but they haven't found—" Her face crumpled, and she wept.

Haven't found his body. Foster completed the sentence in his head.

"Haven't found what, Mom? What haven't they found?"

"Shut up, Ricky!" Evelyn cried. "Just shut up! Can't you see—" Sobbing, she ran from the room.

Foster stared after her, then looked back to his parents. His father still gazed woodenly straight ahead, but his mother's grief-filled eyes met his with a silent plea.

"Come on, Ricky," Foster said, and he practically dragged the protesting younger boy out of the room.

"You're hurting my arm, Foss! Let go! Where are you taking me? Why's everybody crying?"

Foster pushed his brother out the back door. "You know why!" he said, a surge of anger almost blinding him. He clenched his teeth and propelled his brother to the hideout the little boys had made behind the bushes near the shed. Ricky scrambled under the low branches, and Foster ducked down and followed him.

"Now, tell me—"

"No, *you* tell *me,*" Foster said harshly. "You tell me what 'missing' means." He had never come so close to hating his younger brother.

Ricky blinked and said, "You don't know where something is. Or somebody. They never saw Mel after a battle and they don't know where he is and they say 'missing' because they never found—" He stopped and stared at Foster.

The blank look on Ricky's face made Foster think of Father, and he grabbed his brother by the shoulders and shook him hard. "Say it, Ricky! Say it!"

"Because they never found his body! Now lay off me, Foss!"

A wave of emotion swept over Foster as he released his brother. *Mel's body.* He squeezed his eyes shut and saw the mound under the blankets on the bed opposite his bunk. *Mel's body.* He felt his older brother behind him, adjusting his grip on the football, guiding his arm as he threw it. And then he saw the picture in *Life*—one he'd looked at weeks before, the one showing an arm that rose above a wave on the open sea.

Foster buried his face in his arms. Not Mel, he screamed silently. Not my brother Mel!

When he awoke the next morning, Foster's head felt muzzy, and for a moment he thought he must be getting sick—and on a Saturday, too. But then he remembered. Mel. Mel was missing. Foster flopped over and put his head under the pillow where it was dark and quiet. And stuffy. Maybe if he concentrated on the dark stuffiness he wouldn't think about—

A touch on his arm made Foster jump, and then his pillow was pulled aside and he saw Ricky standing on the bunk ladder, peering at him.

"What's wrong, Foss? How come you're still in bed?"

Foster stared at his brother. What was the matter with that kid, anyway? He knew very well what was wrong. Then, shocked that his first thought was something Father might have said, Foster muttered, "You've got your polo shirt on backward again."

"Where is everybody, Foss? When I couldn't find you, I thought I was the only one home, and I'm not supposed to stay home by myself."

Foster sighed. "Evelyn's gone with the other high school kids to pick produce at one of the truck farms, Father's gone to work, and it's Mom's Saturday to volunteer at the hospital," he recited. "Come on, let's get some breakfast."

A few minutes later, the boys were at the table. "'Wheaties, Breakfast of Champions,'" Ricky read from the cereal box. "If our soldiers eat Wheaties, we'll win the war. Do you think they—Hey, Foss, do burglars go to the bathroom?"

"Everybody goes to the bathroom, you dope! What does that have to do with—" Foster broke off, suddenly aware that someone had flushed the toilet.

"It's him!" Ricky cried. "What if he finds out we're still in our pajamas? Then what? He says we have to dress before breakfast."

"He's not coming in here, Ricky. He's gone back to the bedroom."

The boys hurriedly finished their cereal and went to their room to dress. "Better straighten that bedspread," Foster said over his shoulder when he left to answer a knock at the front door.

It was Vic. "I borrowed a couple of buckets," he said, "so we can go on over to the lot and start making our mud balls."

Foster had completely forgotten about the war game. "Wait a minute while I get something." He ran to his closet and dug out his gear, even the canteen Mel had given him, and stuffed it all into the knapsack.

Back at the door he thrust the knapsack at Vic and said, "You'll have to be the general from now on, 'cause I'm not playing anymore. Mel's—" Foster took a deep breath and forced himself to say, "Mel's missing in action. An officer came and told us last night."

"Gosh, Foss, I'm real sorry." Vic said, backing away. "I'll take good care of your stuff."

Foster was watching the other boy walk away when Ricky came up behind him and asked, "So what are we going to do today?"

Foster didn't want to do anything. "Why don't you go play with Sandy?" he suggested.

"I'd rather stay here with you, Foss. What do you want to do?"

Foster took a deep breath and said, "I guess I'll read to Mr. Green."

"And I'll come along. Don't worry, I'll be quiet."

Foster followed Ricky across the yard, wondering if he was too young to understand about Mel. Last night he'd seemed to understand. Last night, he'd been upset, but now—

"It's Saturday," Ricky announced when Mr. Green answered their knock. "Can I play with the toy soldiers again? Can I?"

Smiling, the old man reached for the box that held the tin soldiers his son had played with more than forty years before. Foster liked the way Mr. Green was patient with Ricky, the way he never told him to ask 'may I' instead of 'can I.'

"Foster?"

"Huh? I mean, what did you say?"

Mr. Green gestured to the table where the chess set was set up and said, "I was asking if you would like to finish our game before we read the magazine."

Foster nodded. Maybe it would keep him from thinking about Mel. He moved his knight and frowned when it was captured by a bishop. Why hadn't he seen that?

"Did you hear me, Foster?" Mr. Green gestured to the board and said, "I have finished my turn."

Embarrassed, Foster moved quickly, and to his dismay he heard the old man say, "Checkmate."

"I should have paid better attention," Foster muttered as they began setting up the board for the next day's game.

"Is something troubling you this morning, my young friend?"

Without looking up, Foster nodded. "It's Mel. He's missing in action."

"I am so sorry to hear that. In the other war, my wife and I received the same news about our boy."

Ricky looked up from the mock battle he had set up with the tin soldiers and asked, "Did they ever find him? Or did they just find his body?"

Stunned, Foster thought, Maybe Rick *did* understand. But if he understood, how come he didn't seem worried about Mel?

"Ronald had been taken prisoner," Mr. Green explained, "and when the war was over, he was returned to us."

"I hope we get to see Mel before the war's over," Ricky said, " 'cause our teacher says it's going to last a long time."

Foster stared at his brother, watched him move one row of tin soldiers toward the other just as though there was no such thing as *missing* or *killed.* He heard Mr. Green say quietly, "Sometimes one can say the words without understanding their meaning, Foster."

Maybe that was it, Foster thought, reaching for the most recent issue of *Life.* The article he chose was a long one, and when he came to the end, he realized that he didn't remember a word of what he'd read. "I guess Ricky and I had better go now," he said, standing up.

Mr. Green struggled to his feet and said, "You will have to hope for the best and keep your mind occupied with other things until you have more news about your brother."

Foster nodded, wondering if there would ever be any news at all. He clenched his jaw and blinked to erase the mental image of a flaming plane that spiraled downward, trailing a plume of smoke.

Back at home, as the boys spread peanut butter and jelly for their sandwiches, Ricky asked, "What about him?"

"What about who?"

"You know. Him." Ricky pointed in the direction of their parents' room.

Foster stopped with his knife in midair. When he was sick, Mom brought him cocoa and toast with jam for lunch. "I guess you'd better put some bread in the toaster while I heat water for tea," he said reluctantly. Father never drank cocoa.

"You're the one that's going to take it to him, right, Foss?"

Foster nodded. He had to, for Mom. Had to help the household run smoothly while she volunteered at the hospital. She must be doing what Mr. Green had said, Foster decided—keeping her mind occupied while they waited to hear about Mel.

A few minutes later Foster started down the hall to

his parents' room, carefully balancing a tray, but no matter how hard he tried to keep it steady, some of the tea splashed into the saucer. He hesitated outside the closed door, then swallowed hard and called, "Father? I've brought you some lunch."

After a long pause, a flat voice said, "I'm not hungry. Go away."

Foster retreated to the kitchen and set down the tray, splashing more tea into the saucer. "He said he didn't want anything." Foster said.

"Maybe he's sick to his stomach. Maybe he's afraid he'll throw up."

Mr. Green must be right, Foster thought, because if Ricky really understood what "missing" meant, he'd know why Father hadn't wanted any lunch.

"We'll have to eat the toast and jam so it doesn't go to waste," Ricky said, lifting half the triangles off the plate. "The rest are yours, and you can drink the tea, too."

Why not? That's what Mel would have done. So what if Father said tea was for adults? Foster poured the tea into a glass and went to the Frigidaire for ice, then rummaged in the drawer until he found a long-handled spoon. He stirred in a little sugar, listening to the clink of ice cubes against the glass.

When lunch was over, Foster said, "I have an idea, Ricky—why don't you work on your hideout for a while?" He held his breath until he saw his brother's face light up. Now if only that would keep him occupied all afternoon, Foster thought, envying his father's solitude. *He'd* like to be able to say 'Go away' once in a while.

He had finished rinsing the dishes and was wiping the crumbs from the counter when he heard the mailman call a cheery greeting to the neighbor across the street. Foster reached the front door just as Mr. Mason stepped onto the porch.

"Hi, Foster! Brought you a couple of letters from your brother overseas," the mailman said cheerfully. "One for you and one for your folks."

Foster's head spun as he stared down at the familiar handwriting with its backward slant.

"Hey, are you all right?" the mailman asked, concern in his voice.

Foster didn't feel all right. He didn't really feel anything at all, but he gave a quick nod and turned to go inside.

Automatically, Foster put the letter to his parents on the table by his father's easy chair before he ran to his room, his own letter clutched in his hand. He climbed the ladder to the top bunk, where he tore open the envelope and stared at the page, imagining his brother bent over his tablet, his wrist hooked and the pencil held tightly in his left hand. At last the words came into focus, and Foster began to read.

Dear Foster,

Enjoyed hearing about the Old Man's reaction to Ricky being a Jap in your war game. That was quite a story, kid. Maybe you'll grow up to be a writer. What do you think?

Now pay attention, little brother, 'cause there's something I've got to tell you. We're going to win this REAL war, but it's going to be a long, hard fight, and a lot of American boys are going to die before it's over.

If I'm one of the ones that doesn't make it home again, remember that I joined up of my own free will and that I came here to help do a job that had to be done. Keep on looking out for Ricky the way I always looked out for you, and do whatever you can to make things easier for Mom.

Put this letter away someplace where you can find it if you need it, and I promise the next one will be more cheerful.

Keep your letters coming, Foster, 'cause they help me remember why all of us are over here trying to win this stinking war.

> Love from your soldier brother,
> Mel

Long before he came to the end of the letter, Foster was reading through a blur of tears. He choked back a cry and buried his face in the pillow, cradling its softness in his arms.

He didn't know how long he'd lain there, his body racked by muffled sobs, when he sensed someone beside him. Foster steeled himself for Ricky's string of questions, but the silence grew heavier. Raising his head, he saw his father standing beside him, an empty envelope in his hand.

Foster stared. His father's face was stubbled, his hair disheveled, and he was still in his pajamas. Rumpled blue ones.

"He—wrote to you?"

Wiping his eyes, Foster said, "There's a letter for you and Mom, too. I'll get it."

Father looked—and sounded—as old as Mr. Green, maybe even older, Foster thought as he ran down the hall. When he came back with the letter, Father was gone and the door to his room was closed again. Foster hesitated in the hall, then knocked and said, "I'll slide the letter under your door."

He slipped it through the crack, leaving one corner showing on his side. Almost immediately, he heard the pad of slippers, and the envelope disappeared. Foster went back to his room and stood on tiptoes to reach the shoe box on the shelf in the closet. He started to take it to his bunk, but instead he set it on Mel's bed, sat down beside it, and lifted out his collection of letters from his brother.

He was reading through them all for the second time when his mother came into the room and sat down beside him. "I see that you saved his letters, too," she said. Her voice trembled as she added, "It's hard to imagine that we might never—"

"One came for you today," interrupted Foster. "Father has it." He watched his mother hurry down the hall, taking off her Red Cross nurse cap as she went, and then he went back to his letters.

CHAPTER
21

I t was almost bedtime when Foster looked up from his book and thought how peaceful the evening had been without Father sitting in his easy chair like a ticking time bomb. Not that he wasn't sorry for how bad his father felt, but—

"Mom, there's something I don't understand," Evelyn said, closing her algebra book with a snap. "Why is Father taking this so hard when he refused to talk about Mel and didn't even bother to read his letters?"

"He read those letters, Evelyn. I always left them on my bureau, and I know he read them because I deliberately mixed up the pages, and they were always in the right order the next day."

Evelyn's eyes widened in surprise. "But he barely spoke to Mel when he was home on leave."

"And before Mel joined up, Father was always after him," Foster added, "always punishing him for something." For something he hadn't done, usually.

Mrs. Simmons sighed. "That's part of the reason he's taking this so hard, as Evelyn put it."

"I didn't think Father even liked Mel," Ricky said, and the others nodded their agreement.

Mrs. Simmons took a few more stitches on the shirt she was mending before she said quietly, "Your father thought the sun rose and set on that boy. He was hard on him because he had great plans for his future—a scholarship to the university, a good job when he graduated—but instead of helping Mel get ahead in life, he drove him away."

"You knew?" Foster asked. "Knew that Mel joined up to get away from Father?"

"Of course I knew! Do you think I'm blind? Do you think I don't see that all of you are terrified of your father? That you avoid him any way you can, whether it's escaping into the service like Mel did or into your own little world the way you do?"

Foster stared at his mother. Was that what he did?

His mother's voice grew hard as she asked, "You don't really think your father doesn't notice, do you? How do you think it makes him feel to work as hard as he does to be a good provider, and to try as hard as he does to bring all of you up to be decent people, and then to see the bunch of you use any excuse you can find to stay out of his way? How do you think it makes *me* feel?"

By now, tears were flowing down her cheeks, and Foster felt shaken. He'd never thought about how his mother must feel—or about how his father felt, either. He'd never really thought about grown-ups' feelings at all, except maybe Mr. Green's.

"Are you listening to me, Foster?"

"Yes, ma'am!"

"Good, because all of you need to hear what I'm about to tell you," his mother said, in control of herself again. "It broke your father's heart when Mel quit school, when he enlisted before he earned his high school diploma."

Evelyn frowned. "But Father never finished high school, either, so why—"

"Your father had to leave school after the eighth grade to support his widowed mother and his younger sisters," Mrs. Simmons interrupted, "and he wants his sons to have the opportunities he never had. To have a chance at better jobs and a better life."

"What about his daughter? What about me and my life? And why's he been so hard on me lately?" challenged Evelyn.

Mrs. Simmons said quietly, "Because he doesn't want you to end up like his sister Edna."

Aunt Edna had run off with a handsome but no-good salesman and had a baby "too soon," whatever that meant, Foster remembered. Now she was saddled with an alcoholic husband and had to take in ironing to help provide for their six children.

"Edna wasn't much older than you when she ran off and got married, and every time your father sees you with a boy, he thinks of that."

"Well, I'm certainly not about to run off and get married and have a bunch of kids," Evelyn declared.

With a faint smile, her mother said, "Then that's one less thing to worry about. I—"

Her words were cut off by the wail of sirens, and Foster quickly clicked off the floor lamp. Another alert, not an air raid, he told himself. It's just an alert, he repeated silently, but still his heart pounded.

"I'll have to patrol the neighborhood for him," Mrs. Simmons said, already on her way to get Father's warden gear.

"Come on, Ricky, let's sit in the kitchen," Foster said, thinking of the protection the table would provide if it turned out to be an air raid instead of an alert.

Ricky followed his brother so closely that he kept walking on Foster's heels, and when he saw their mother putting on the warden helmet, he ran and clung to her, crying so loudly he almost drowned out the blaring sirens. "Don't go, Mom! I don't want you to be bombed! Please, don't—"

"Let go of me, Ricky," she said sharply. "I have a job to do."

"It's my job, Ruby. Take off that helmet."

In the flickering light of the candle Evelyn had lit, Foster saw that his father had pulled slacks and a sweater over his pajamas. Without a word, Mom hung the whistle around his neck and settled the helmet on his head while he slid the armband over his sleeve. As Father started for the door, Foster thought he looked smaller, somehow.

As soon as the front door shut behind him, Evelyn said, "Are you sure he should be going out, Mom? He looks perfectly awful."

"This is the best thing that could have happened," Mrs. Simmons said, drawing Ricky close to her. "There's nothing like responsibilities to keep a person going."

"What's the matter with him, Mom?" Ricky asked, sniffling.

"Oh, for Pete's sake, Ricky," Evelyn snapped, "what do you *think* is the matter with him?"

Ignoring her daughter, Mrs. Simmons said, "Your father's worried about Mel, dear."

"He doesn't have to worry about Mel," Ricky said confidently. "Mel's alive."

In the stunned silence that followed his brother's words, Foster found himself feeling almost hopeful for the first time. After all, the officer said "missing." He didn't say "killed." Hesitantly, Foster asked, "Do you think believing Mel's alive can help?"

His mother sighed as she sat down at the kitchen table. "It certainly can't do any harm."

But Evelyn said flatly, "Nothing can change what's already happened. If Mel's dead, it won't matter what you believe, and it won't make a bit of difference that all those people from church are praying for him."

But it might make a difference if he's still alive, Foster thought. It might help him if he's wounded, or if he's been captured. Somehow, it made Foster feel a little better to know that people were praying for his brother.

The house was so quiet the next afternoon that Foster could hear the hum of the kitchen clock. He'd been glad when Sandy invited Ricky to play, glad that Vic was busy with chores. Foster closed his book. He'd wanted some time to himself, but now that he had it, he felt terribly alone.

He looked across the kitchen table, and his throat felt tight when his eyes came to rest on Mel's chair. Why did it suddenly look so—empty? Foster pushed his own chair away from the table and stumbled to his room.

"I'll write to Jimmy," he whispered, trying to forget that none of his other letters had been answered, trying not to think that he might never again write a letter to Mel.

Dear Jimmy,

    Something awful has happened. Mel is missing in action. We got the news a week ago, and now we're waiting to hear something more. Mom says we might not hear anything for months. I'm pretty sure she thinks he's dead. I don't know what I think.

The truth was, he didn't want to think, and he didn't want to write about it anymore, either. Somehow, putting the words down on paper made it all seem more real. Foster signed his name and addressed an envelope, but instead of folding the letter he sat and stared at it for a long time. Finally, he added a postscript:

    P.S. I guess you'll feel bad that Mel is missing because of the Japanese, just like I feel bad that your dad was taken to jail and you were sent away to the desert by the American government. But that doesn't make any difference to our being friends.

Foster read over what he had written. That last sentence didn't sound right, but he didn't know any other way to say it. Besides, Jimmy would know what he meant.

After Foster mailed the letter he went next door to read to Mr. Green. " 'Victory at Midway: Tides of War Change as America Wins Air and Sea Battle,' " he read as he glanced through the latest issue of *Life*. "Want to hear that one?"

"It will be good to hear about a victory, after so much bad news these past months," the old man said, leaning back in his chair.

Foster began the article, and the further he read, the more excited he became. His voice faded away as his eyes raced down the page. "When was this battle, anyway?" he muttered. Heart pounding, he skimmed the beginning of the article looking for the dates.

"It started June fourth. I'll bet Mel was in this battle," he said, his voice tense. Maybe his brother had helped to make it a victory! He tried not to think that his brother might have died to make it a victory.

Foster began to read again. "Listen to this," he said, his voice shaking. "They're still sending planes out every day to look for downed fliers, and they've found some of them drifting along in rafts." Missing fliers had been found! Maybe Mel— "How long do you think somebody could float in one of those rafts and still be alive?"

"It would depend on how much fresh water he had, and on whether he had been wounded," Mr. Green said quietly.

He thinks Mel's dead. Foster's hopes fell, and to break the awkward silence he turned to the article again. "It says here that we sank four of their aircraft carriers and shot down 253 of their planes, and we only lost one carrier, a destroyer, and 147 planes." Shaken, he looked up and whispered, " 'Only' 147 planes?"

Mr. Green sighed heavily. "Our losses were fewer than those of the enemy, but each life lost brings sorrow to loved ones at home. Perhaps the writer did not want to think of that."

Foster closed the magazine and set it on the table. "I have to go now," he said, trying to keep his voice steady. He bolted for home as the words "only 147 planes lost" echoed in his mind. He was sure that Mel had been on one of them.

CHAPTER
22

The classroom hummed with subdued excitement as the hands of the clock crept toward noon and the students cleaned out their desks or helped Mrs. Jackson. Pam was washing the board, and Wilbur had taken the erasers outside to clap against the building where they would leave white rectangles that would last till it rained. Jenny and some of the other girls were dismantling the bulletin boards, and Vic was alternately sweeping the floor and poking people with the broom handle.

Foster had already cleaned out his desk, returned the textbooks—and the class library book he'd thought was lost—and dumped all his papers in the trash can. Now there was nothing for him to do but wait for the class to be dismissed. On the playground at recess, some of the kids had already been chanting "No more pencils, no more books, no more teachers' dirty looks," but Foster hadn't joined in. This year, the last day of school was just another day of waiting to hear about Mel.

At least school helped pass the time, Foster thought. It occupied his mind so he didn't always think about Mel, wondering what had happened to him, wondering if he—

"Boys and girls? Boys and girls!" Mrs. Jackson's voice broke into Foster's thoughts, and he saw that she was standing behind her desk with a stack of envelopes. When everyone was quiet, she said, "This class has had a fine year, and now it's time for me to wish you a good summer. When the bell rings at noon, I want you to file out of the room row by row, just as you did for the air-raid drills, so that I can give each of you your report card and a good-bye handshake. Remember, the envelope is addressed to your parents, so you are not to open it."

Maybe that would keep the guys from trying to make Wilbur show them his report, Foster thought, hoping the other boy had passed. He was too big to be held back again. The bell rang, and Foster could hear the kids from the other classrooms burst into the hall, cheering, but he was glad Mrs. Jackson was doing it this way.

"Good-bye, Foster, and good luck," the teacher said, smiling as she gave him his report card and shook his hand.

"Bye," he said, suddenly feeling bashful. He'd never touched a teacher before.

Vic and Jenny were waiting for him in the hall, and the excitement on their faces stirred Foster's memory of other last days of school. He grinned, and the three of them began to chant, "No more pencils, no more books, no more . . ."

It felt strange not to rush back to school as soon as he finished lunch, Foster thought after he had put the milk bottle in the Frigidaire. Not knowing quite what to do with himself, he went outside to water the victory garden. After he had carefully coiled the hose and placed it under the spigot, Foster muttered, "Guess I'll check the mailbox."

His heart leaped when he saw the familiar schoolboy writing on the envelope. Jimmy! "He finally wrote back," Foster whispered as he sank down on the porch step and ripped into the envelope.

Dear Foster,

I'm sorry your brother is missing, and no matter what you say I'm sorry that it's because of the Japanese. But I guess you're right that it doesn't have anything to do with you and me, and neither does what the U.S. government has done. I'm still mad about being sent to this place and about my dad being kept in jail all that time for no reason at all. They finally let him come here, so we're all to-gether again.

My mother told me how you brought her gro-ceries. Both my parents send their greetings.

This place is huge with rows and rows of bar-racks and more still being built. Each family has one room to live in. Jill's is next door to ours. She says hi.

The worst things about this place are the barbed-wire fence around it and the guards with guns, the heat, the sand, always standing in lines, the food at the dining hall, and no privacy. The best things are being with so many other Japanese-Americans and the view of the mountains.

I'm sorry I didn't write before, and I'm glad you still want to be friends anyhow.

Your friend,
Jimmy

p.s. Tell me when you get any news about Mel.

Foster's heart sang. Clutching the letter, he ran next door calling, "Mr. Green? Mr. Green!"

When the old man saw Foster's joyful expression and the envelope in his hand, he exclaimed, "Your brother is safe, then! That is wonderful news. You must come in and read me the letter."

Foster's excitement drained away. "It's not news about Mel," he said. "It's just a letter from Jimmy. I—I wanted you to know that he'd finally written back to me." Now, though, it didn't seem important after all.

"That, too, is wonderful news, and it deserves a celebration." Mr. Green motioned for Foster to follow him into the kitchen, where he took a bottle of ginger ale from the Frigidaire. "If you will find two glasses in the cupboard," he said, "we will celebrate friendship—yours and Jimmy's."

And yours and mine, too, Foster said silently, wishing he could say the words aloud. He set the glasses on the counter and watched the bubbles rise as the old man poured the golden liquid.

CHAPTER
23

"H ey, Foss," Vic said, looking up from the game the boys were playing on his shady front porch. "Look there."

Following Vic's gaze, Foster saw a man slowly pedal past, checking the house numbers on the other side of the street. The man coasted to a stop in front of Foster's house and glanced down at the yellow envelope in his hand, then swung off the bike and limped toward the door.

Foster dropped his cards and ran home. "I'll take that," he said, reaching for the envelope. His throat felt dry as he stared at the words WESTERN UNION TELEGRAM centered in large letters above the "window" where the address showed through. This was it, Foster thought, his heart pounding. Mel wasn't missing anymore, and he was about to find out if—

"Sign here, kid," the man said, pointing, and Foster managed to scrawl his name on the line. He went inside before he tore open the envelope and pulled out the telegram to read the message that had been pasted on in strips:

IT HAS NOW BEEN OFFICIALLY ESTABLISHED FROM REPORTS RECEIVED BY THE WAR DEPART-MENT THAT YOUR SON SERGEANT MELVIN ANDREW SIMMONS WAS KILLED IN ACTION ON 4 JUNE IN THE SERVICE OF HIS COUNTRY THE SEC-RETARY OF WAR EXTENDS HIS DEEPEST SYMPATHY CONFIRMING LETTER FOLLOWS

Foster stared at the words until they ran together. Blindly, he stumbled into the living room and put the telegram on the table by Father's easy chair. His feet carried him down the hall to his room, where he threw himself onto Mel's bed. Clutching his brother's pillow, he sobbed until he fell into an exhausted sleep.

The afternoon sun was streaming in the bedroom window when Foster woke. His head felt like it was packed with cotton, and when he sat up he saw that the tufts on the chenille bedspread had made a pattern of indentations on his skin.

Before the telegram came, Foster had thought it would be easier once he knew the truth about his brother, but it wasn't. The truth was like a heavy weight bearing down on him. Slowly he got up and smoothed the bedspread. He washed his face with cold water, which made him look better, at least, and then he wandered aimlessly around the house.

In the living room, Foster found himself drawn toward the yellow rectangle on the table by Father's chair. Mom would see it first, and then she'd know, too, and it would be even worse for her than it was for him, and she'd have to tell Ricky when he came home from his school friend's house at suppertime. Or maybe Rick would come home early and *he'd* have to—

Foster's hand shot out, and the next thing he knew, he was clutching the telegram and racing to his room. His heart pounded as he wrenched open the closet door and reached for the box of letters. He would bury the hateful yellow envelope among Mel's letters and pretend it had never come.

That was better, Foster thought after he closed the door with more force than necessary. He took a deep breath and squared his shoulders. Mrs. Jackson had been right when she'd told the class they would feel better if they stood up straight.

Suddenly aware that he was hungry, Foster grabbed his library book from the desk and headed for the kitchen to fix a sandwich. He was enjoying the luxury of reading while he ate instead of listening to Ricky's chatter when he heard a knock.

Mr. Green! "Come on in," Foster said, opening the screen door wide.

"My neighbor on the other side just told me she saw a Western Union messenger stop at your house this morning," the old man said, "and I have come to make sure that you are all right."

The telegram. How could he have thought he could pretend it had never come? Pretend he didn't know that Mel was—Foster dashed to his room and pulled the box of letters from the closet. He emptied it onto Mel's bed and was reaching for the yellow envelope that stood out among all the white ones when he looked up and saw that Mr. Green had followed him. Shame and confusion washed over Foster. How could he ever explain the incredibly stupid thing he had done?

"It was bad news, then; news too terrible to accept at first. I am so sorry, Foster." Mr. Green waited while Foster busied himself with gathering up the scattered letters. When he had closed the box and put it back on the closet shelf, Mr. Green asked gently. "Shall we put the telegram where your parents will find it this evening?"

His eyes downcast, Foster nodded. "I didn't want Mom to have to know," he whispered, blinking back tears. *He* didn't want to have to know, either.

"I think this will only confirm what your mother already knows in her heart. It will allow her to bring one chapter of her life to a close so she can begin the next."

She'd close the Mel chapter. Maybe she could go back and read over it later when— "Huh?"

"I asked if you would like me to wait here with you until your mother returns."

Foster shook his head. "I'll be all right now." He watched from the door until Mr. Green reached the sidewalk, and then he went to the kitchen and choked down the rest of his lunch. If it weren't wrong to waste food, he'd have thrown it out.

He tried to read, but he couldn't keep his mind on the story. Closing the book, he wondered what he was going to do for the rest of the afternoon, and then he remembered—Jimmy had said to let him know when they heard anything. Foster walked purposefully back to his room, relieved that he'd found a way to escape the emptiness he was feeling. For a little while, at least.

> *Dear Jimmy,*
>
> *We found out about Mel. Today we got a telegram that said he was*

Foster's hand faltered, and he wasn't sure he could bring himself to write the word. He started to crumple the paper so he wouldn't have to, but then he whispered, "No." Picking up his pen—the one Mel had given him for Christmas—Foster forced himself to write *killed in action June 4.*

He stared at the inky blue loops of the word "killed" until the page became a blur, and then he blinked it back into focus. There it was—the plain and simple truth, the truth he'd suspected all along but had dreaded hearing, the truth he'd tried to deny by hiding the telegram. And now he had faced it.

But this was only the beginning, he thought numbly. He would have to face it again tomorrow, and the next day, and the next. Every day for the rest of his life.

Dinner the next evening seemed to drag on forever. Foster's stomach told him he was hungry, but everything tasted so dry he could hardly swallow.

"What is this, Mom?" Ricky asked. "You never made it before."

"It's a chicken potpie Sandy and Vic's mother brought over," Mrs. Simmons answered. "And the molded salad is from Mrs. Hatter, down the street. That lettuce is from our victory garden, by the way, Horace," Mother added, but Father didn't seem to hear her.

Ricky lifted the flaky crust from his serving of potpie, and when that brought no reprimand from Father, Foster began to dissect his jello salad, carefully removing all the pineapple chunks. He wondered why Mrs. Hatter's jello was so rubbery.

"With all the food folks have brought, I won't have to cook for a week," Mrs. Simmons said. "The other volunteers at the hospital must have pooled their sugar ration to make that big sheet cake."

Foster hoped the cake would taste better than the rest of the food people had brought after they heard about the telegram. He wondered if anything would ever taste good again. If anything would ever be the same again. No, it couldn't be. Mel's chair would always be empty, and—*Mel's chair was gone.* Across the table, Evelyn sat halfway between her parents instead of next to Mom with Mel's empty chair beside her. Foster sent his own chair crashing to the floor as he leaped up from the table and raced to his room. His legs seemed to dissolve beneath him when he saw that Mel's bed was still there. He threw himself down on it and hugged the pillow to him, but the tears didn't come until his mother sat down beside him and he felt her hand on his shoulder.

"Are you all right, son?"

His face still buried in the pillow, Foster said, "Somebody took Mel's chair away, and I was afraid they might have taken his bed, too."

"I moved the chair, Foster, and it was the hardest thing I've ever done." His mother's voice trembled, and she paused for a moment. "Taking away that chair was my way of accepting that he's—gone."

Gone. What a forlorn word it was, what a final word. "Just don't take away his bed," Foster whispered. "Okay, Mom?"

"It might be easier for you and Ricky if we moved it," she said gently. "Then we could take the bunks apart and you boys could use them as twin beds."

Foster sat up. "You can't do that—Ricky wouldn't be able to sleep! He has to be in the bottom bunk because that's like being under the table," he explained. "You know, like in an air raid you're supposed to get under a table so you'll be safe."

Tears filled his mother's eyes and she whispered, "I've been so wrapped up in worrying about Mel that I never realized what this war was doing to my other sons." She gave Foster a quick hug and left the room.

CHAPTER
24

Foster looked at the thriving tomato plants and wished he could be as excited about them as Jenny was. He gave a start when he realized that she was asking him something.

"Don't you think so, Foster?" she repeated.

"Yeah, sure!" What was he agreeing to?

"Hey, Jenny, can I water the tomatoes? Can I?" Ricky asked.

"I watered them this morning," she said.

"Then how about those little plants over there? Can I water them instead? Tell her how I always water our plants, Foster."

Jenny said, "I already watered the whole victory garden, okay, Ricky?"

"Okay," Ricky said cheerfully, and he settled down to watch some ants streaming in and out of an anthill.

Turning to Foster, Jenny said quietly, "Vic told me you found out about your brother. I'm really sorry."

"Yeah. Until we heard he was missing, I'd never thought much about something happening to Mel." Foster tried to push away the uneasy feeling that he might have been playing war with the kids at the exact time Mel's plane went down. Today was Tuesday, so June 4 would have been a—Thursday, and they only played the war game on weekends. Relief flooded through him.

"Are you okay? You look kind of funny."

Flustered, Foster changed the subject. "Listen, Jenny, my mom said maybe some of us could collect stuff for the kids in the children's ward at the hospital. You know, puzzles and games and things like that."

Jenny seemed relieved to be talking about something else. "We could gather up all our old comic books, too," she said enthusiastically. "I've got lots of comics."

Foster thought of the hours he and Jimmy had spent reading comics. What had become of Jimmy's collection? He probably wished he had it with him, since there wasn't much to do in that internment camp.

He heard Jenny say, "You look like you just had an idea—I can almost see a cartoon lightbulb flashing over your head."

"Listen, Jenny, how about if we collect some stuff for Jimmy Osaki and his friends? The kids in the hospital where Mom works have visitors, and they know they'll be going home before too long, but those internment camps are in the middle of nowhere, and the people there don't know how long they'll have to stay."

Jenny frowned and asked, "You mean send things to the Japs?"

"The kids are Americans," Foster said quickly. "My mom says they're 'Americans of Japanese ancestry,' just like people in our family are 'Americans of British ancestry.'"

"But we aren't fighting the British, Foster."

"Not this time."

Jenny gave him a long, searching look and finally said, "Well, all right, but I don't think we'd better advertise who we're collecting for."

Foster began to feel uncomfortable. He didn't like the idea of tricking people about something like that. But then he remembered what his mother had said about answering Jill's letter. "We could put up a sign that says we're collecting stuff for the peace effort," he suggested hopefully.

Before Jenny could reply, they heard shouting and ran to the sidewalk. Down the street came a newsboy with his wagon full of papers, and he was hollering, "Extra! Extra! Read all about it—Nazi saboteurs caught on East Coast beach! Read all about it!" An old man came outside and waved for the newsboy to stop, and further down the block a woman with a red apron over her dress called for him to wait.

"I think people's minds are on the war effort right now, Foster," Jenny said, "but we could go through our own stuff. I wouldn't mind if we sent things to Jimmy Osaki, since he was a friend of yours. Hey, I have an idea—let's read over all our comic books before we send them."

The newsboy's singsong voice grated on Foster's ears, and suddenly the idea of escaping into the world of Superman and Batman seemed like a good way to forget about the war, to forget that he'd never see Mel again. Foster thought of the neat stacks of comics on the bottom shelf of his bookcase and said, "I'll go home and get all my comics. See you in a little while."

Half an hour later, Foster and Ricky were back at Jenny's house with a wagonload of comics, and the three of them settled down on the glider at the shady end of the front porch. "Don't rock, Ricky," Jenny said. "You're making me seasick."

As Foster thumbed through Jenny's pile, he was beginning to think that they were all Wonder Woman when he came across some Blackhawk comic books. To his delight, there were several issues he'd never read, and he settled down with them.

"Ricky! Didn't you hear me ask you not to rock the glider?" Jenny's voice was cross.

"He can't help it, Jenny, he's just a jittery kind of kid," Foster said, adding, "Rick, if you want to stay here and look at comics with us, you'd better sit in one of those chairs." As he watched Ricky move reluctantly to one of the red metal porch chairs, Foster decided it was a good thing his brother didn't realize that he *had* to stay there with them. For the hundredth time that summer, Foster reminded himself that he was looking after Ricky for the war effort, and then he turned back to the exploits of the aviator hero, Blackhawk.

"Now *you're* rocking the glider," Jenny said.

"Sorry," Foster mumbled, wondering why he'd never noticed the menacing expressions on the faces of the enemy pilots Blackhawk was shooting down. Had Mel ever been close enough to see the faces of the Japs in the planes that were shooting at his bomber? Had he seen the face of the one who— "Sorry," Foster said again when Jenny gave a long, drawn-out sigh and moved from the glider to the chair next to Ricky's. He hadn't been aware that he was rocking the glider again, and rocking it hard.

Maybe Mel's bomber hadn't been shot down by a plane at all, maybe it was downed by anti-aircraft fire, Foster thought as he tossed aside the Blackhawk comic and reached for a Wonder Woman. At least there shouldn't be any battles or Japs in this one, he thought, folding back the cover. But he hadn't read many pages before a sinister-looking spy, the slant of his eyes exaggerated, made his appearance.

Foster dropped the magazine and reached for one of Ricky's Walt Disney comics. He didn't need to be reminded of the Japs, to be reminded of the war, to be reminded that Mel—

"What's the matter?" Jenny asked. "Are you thinking about your brother?"

"All these comics are full of Japs," Foster complained.

"So are these," said Jenny. "We'd better make two piles, one with Jap characters and one without, 'cause I don't think Jimmy and the other kids want to read comics about enemy Japs."

"Let's just send all the comics to the children's ward at the hospital," Foster said. "I don't feel like sorting through them." He didn't feel much like doing anything at all.

Jenny closed her magazine and joined him on the glider. "Okay. Then what do you want to do?"

Foster stared glumly at his shoes. What else was there to do? The war game was ruined for him, reading comic books was ruined for him, and the long, empty summer loomed ahead. His whole empty life loomed ahead, a life without Mel. Mom had said he should try to keep busy, Foster remembered, so he turned to Jenny and asked, "Do you have any games?"

"Sure. We could play Chinese checkers, or I could bring out some cards and we could play war."

"Chinese checkers," Foster said quickly, "but bring

out the cards, too, in case Ricky wants to make a card house, okay?"

Jenny nodded and disappeared inside, but Ricky called after her, "You don't need to bring the cards—I'll just watch you guys play."

Foster groaned inwardly. He didn't care that it was his contribution to the war effort, he was sick and tired of always having to watch Ricky. And then he remembered: *Keep on looking out for Ricky the way I always looked out for you, and do whatever you can to make things easier for Mom.* He'd read that last letter so many times he knew it by heart, but he'd forgotten anyway.

Foster gave his brother a friendly punch on the arm and said, "You watch real hard, Ricky, and pretty soon you'll be able to play, too. And you know what we're going to do when we go home?"

"What, Foss? What are we going to do?"

"We're going to find my softball, and I'm going to start teaching you to catch and throw," Foster said, adding silently, *Just like Mel taught me. I'll use his mitt, and Rick can use mine. . . .*

The next afternoon Foster paid Vic $2000 for landing on Boardwalk with a hotel and hoped he would soon be bankrupt so he wouldn't have to play any longer. Monopoly had always been his favorite game, but it just wasn't much fun anymore. His head jerked up when he heard a terrible wailing out front.

"Criminy! What's that?" Vic asked.

But Foster was already halfway down the hall. He burst outside and saw Ricky standing on the sidewalk, pointing to the house and sobbing. No blood. Not hit by a car, not bitten by a dog. Foster grabbed his brother by the shoulders. "What's the matter, Rick? What's wrong?" he asked, kneeling in front of him.

Ricky practically collapsed into his arms. "Mel's dead, Foster. Mel's *dead*!" he cried.

Stunned, Foster barely heard Vic say he had to go home, barely noticed the neighbor across the street run around the house still holding her garden clippers. Foster gave Ricky a little shake and said, "You knew that, Rick. The telegram came two days ago."

"But it wasn't true then, and now it is—look!" He pointed toward the house. Foster turned to look, but he didn't understand until Ricky sobbed, "It turned gold, Foster! Mel's star turned gold."

Foster swallowed hard. The night before, he'd awakened long past midnight and seen the glow of a light. He'd tiptoed down the hall and watched from the living room doorway while his mother hung a new service flag in the window, one with a gold star. His throat had ached when she clasped the blue star flag to her and wept. Her tears still flowing, she'd slipped it into her sewing basket, and Foster had crept back to his room.

"Listen, Rick, if you want, I can find that blue star flag for you, and you can keep it."

"So I can always be a Blue Star Brother?" Ricky said, hiccuping.

Foster hesitated. "You can be a Blue Star Brother, but Mel will still be—Mel will still be a gold star. Come on inside now." Foster went to his mother's sewing basket and found the flag at the very bottom, under her button box and pinking shears.

"I'm going to take this with me everywhere I go," Ricky said, sniffling as he reached for it.

Oh, no. Oh, *no*! Foster could still remember how his brother used to refuse to go anywhere without his "banky," the little scrap Mom had cut from his blanket when Father had announced that Ricky was too old to be dragging a blanket around with him. Foster wasn't going to go through something like that again. He could hear it now: I can't leave for school yet, Foss, 'cause I haven't found my blue star.

"How about this," Foster said. "We'll thumbtack it to the bottom of my bunk where you can look up and see it first thing in the morning, and that way you'll always know where it is. Okay?"

"Okay," Ricky agreed. "That way Mel can watch over me at night when I'm scared."

Foster hadn't known his brother was still scared at night. He could always hear Ricky's even breathing when he lay awake as the searchlights crisscrossed the sky and cast eerie patterns on the ceiling in their endless vigilance for enemy planes. For a crazy moment Foster wondered if knowing that the blue star banner was tacked to the bottom of his bunk would make *him* feel better when he waked in the night.

CHAPTER
25

A few days later, Foster was sitting on Mr. Green's front porch, reading aloud, while Ricky ran around and around the house making airplane noises.

The mailman came up the walk and said cheerfully, "Nothing but a bill today, Mr. Green, but somebody wrote you a letter, Foster, and I left some more sympathy cards and a real official-looking envelope for your folks."

Mr. Green winced as the mailman cut across the yard on his way to the next house, and Foster vowed to always use the sidewalk. He began to read again, but the old man stopped him and said, "We can finish the article after you have read your letter, Foster."

"I'll be right back, Mr. Green." Foster dashed down the sidewalk and almost collided with Ricky, who immediately changed from an airplane into a tagalong little brother. Foster reached into the mailbox and pulled out a letter from Jimmy and the large envelope under it. "Hey, Rick, I see six Zeroes flying in low—you'd better shoot 'em down," Foster said, and to his relief, his brother zoomed away.

Jimmy must have written back as soon as he got my letter, Foster thought. His eyes widened when he unfolded the paper and began to study the drawing that covered the page—aircraft carriers and cruisers on the ocean, and a sky filled with planes.

"The Battle of Midway," Foster whispered when he read the names lettered on the ships and saw the pair of tiny islands near the edge of the page. Across the top of the sky were the words, "My parents and I are sorry about your brother. At least the battle was a great victory for America." And in the bottom right corner was Jimmy's signature. This was a whole lot better than all those notes and sympathy cards his parents were getting, Foster thought.

He put Jimmy's letter in his pocket and took the official-looking manila envelope to show Mr. Green. "It's from the War Department," he said. "Hey, do you think maybe they made a mistake?"

Mr. Green said quietly, "I think they would have sent another telegram instead of a letter if there had been a mistake."

Foster's hopes fell as quickly as they had risen. "I'm going to open it," he said. It wasn't addressed to him, but the telegram hadn't been, either, and Mom had been glad he'd read it so she didn't have to tell him the news. Carefully, he opened the large envelope and pulled out a flat piece of paper.

"It's a certificate of some kind," Foster said. He squinted at the Old English type and began to read. "'For military merit and for wounds received in action 4 June 1942, resulting in his death.' Mel's name and some number are written in, and there's a drawing on it that looks like George Washington."

"See if there is anything else in the envelope," Mr. Green said as Ricky taxied in for a landing.

"There's some kind of medal," Foster said, opening a small flat box, "and it has George Washington on it, too, sort of like a cameo on a heart-shaped background."

Mr. Green said quietly, "Wounded soldiers receive the Purple Heart, and your brother's medal has been sent home to his family."

"Can I see it, Foss? Can I see the medal?"

"Okay, but don't take it out of the box."

Ricky traced a finger around the edge of the Purple Heart and then began to march and chant, "Mel won a medal, Mel won a medal."

Raising his voice, Foster shouted, "Cut that out, Ricky!"

But Ricky marched right past him, chanting, "Mel won a medal, Mel won a— Hey!"

"Shut *up,* Rick," Foster said, releasing his brother's arm. "It's not something to brag about. Put this by Father's chair," he added as he slipped the certificate and medal back into the envelope. "And don't cut across the lawn."

Back on Mr. Green's porch he picked up the magazine and muttered, "Now where was I?"

"You were reading about the Russian armies pushing back a new Nazi attack," the old man reminded him, "but perhaps you would rather not read about battles today."

Foster shook his head. Somehow it was a comfort to be here with Mr. Green, to be useful without being in charge, to feel understood without having to explain. He could relax and be himself here, just like he could when he was with Jenny. Settling back in his chair, he began to read.

Later, when Mrs. Simmons came home from working at the hospital, Ricky ran to meet her. "Mel got a medal, Mom! He got a medal!"

Foster was right behind his brother, and he handed Mrs. Simmons the envelope. "It's the Purple Heart," he said.

"These days I never know what will be waiting for me when I come home," she said, sinking down onto the sofa to read the certificate.

Foster thought of the letter that had come from

Mel's commanding officer soon after the telegram arrived. The officer had written that Mel's "good humor and courage made him an inspiration to men many years his senior." And then he had told how Mel's whole crew had been lost when their B-26 burst into flames, witnessed by an airman who had been seriously injured when he returned to base and crash-landed his damaged plane. Until the pilot recovered enough to report this, there had been hope that the crew might be found by the search planes.

"What's going on here? Are you all right, Ruby?"

Foster jumped at the sound of his father's voice, and his mother got to her feet and said, "I'm all right. I was looking at these, so dinner will be a little late tonight." She gave him a hug and handed him the contents of the envelope.

Mr. Simmons looked from the certificate to the Purple Heart. He was still standing in the middle of the living room staring at them when Foster edged his way into the hall.

This is station WAR in San Diego, and we're about to talk to young Foster Simmons again. Foster, we understand that your brother's plane was shot down over the Pacific and that your family has received the Purple Heart he was awarded. Tell me, Foster, why is this medal called the Purple Heart?

I don't know, sir. It ought to be called the Broken Heart.

***

"Honestly, Mom, I think I'd rather listen to Father criticize us all the time than have him just sit here night after night," Evelyn said as she and Foster set the table for supper that evening.

Foster wasn't sure he agreed. It was true that Father hadn't seemed at all like himself since he'd first heard that Mel was missing, but as far as *he* was concerned, the silent, withdrawn shadow of a man he had been since then was an improvement.

"Losing a son has hit him hard," Mrs. Simmons said from the stove.

Her eyes flashing, Evelyn said, "Maybe he should remember that he's got two other sons and a daughter."

"Maybe you should remind him, Evelyn."

This conversation was like a Ping-Pong game, Foster thought, his eyes moving from his mother to his sister and back again. Your turn, Evelyn, he prompted silently.

"Maybe I'll do that," his sister said, just as if she had heard him.

Father came slowly into the kitchen, and as she had done every evening for the past three weeks, Mrs. Simmons waited until everyone was seated at the table and then said, "Let's all join hands and sing our blessing tonight."

And as he did each evening, Foster thought how cold and lifeless Father's hand felt compared to Ricky's small warm one. He was glad when the song was over. Foster watched his father fill the plates and pass them around without looking up, saw his mother frown at the small servings her husband gave himself.

Evelyn's voice broke the silence. "You know, when school starts in the fall, I'll have to decide between the academic program and the commercial program. I was wondering if I could discuss my choice with you, Father."

Foster had almost decided Father wasn't going to answer when at last he said, "You can take whichever one you want, Evelyn."

"Good," Evelyn said brightly. "Then I'll take the academic program so I can go to the university."

Father stared at her. *"You're* going to the university?"

Well, that got his attention, Foster thought, looking at his sister with respect. She sure had taken up Mom's challenge.

Evelyn nodded and said, "If I study hard, maybe I can get a scholarship. What do you think, Father?"

"I think it's strange you have this sudden interest in education. Is that boyfriend of yours—that Brad—thinking about going to college instead of serving his country?"

Father sounded almost like himself again, Foster

thought, and half relieved, half sorry, he waited to hear what Evelyn would say to that.

She ignored the crack about Brad and said, "I guess seeing all the things women are doing nowadays makes getting a good education seem more important."

"Hmph. Taking over. That's what they're doing. Can't go anywhere these days without seeing some woman doing a man's job. I even saw a woman mail-man the other day."

Foster grinned, and his father snapped, "What's so funny, young man?"

Caught off guard, Foster stammered, "I was just wondering why they didn't call a woman mailman a 'fe-mailman'."

There was silence until Ricky laughed. "I get it," he said, putting down his fork, "see, a man's a male, and a woman's a—"

"All right, all right! We get it, too," Father inter-rupted.

Foster glanced at his brother to make sure he hadn't been withered by his father's words and was reassured when the little boy whispered, "That was a good one, Foss."

But Foster barely heard him. He was trying to get used to the idea that no one seemed to be afraid of Father anymore.

CHAPTER
26

Y ou're doing it all wrong, you know."
Foster gave a start and turned to see his father standing on the sidewalk, lunch box in his hand. "Huh?"

"Don't you know you'll never make a decent ballplayer out of Rick if you always throw the ball right to him? You have to make him run forward or backward to catch it and you have to make him run to the left and right, too."

Foster heard Ricky yell, "Heads up, Foss!" and saw him throw the ball in a wild arc. Oh, no. Oh, *no*! He'd never be able to catch that! But to Foster's amazement, his father stepped into the street, caught the ball, and tossed it back with so much force that it sailed high over Ricky's head.

"Gosh, I didn't know you could play ball, Father," Foster said as his brother chased the ball toward the corner.

Father gave him a scornful look and said, "How do you think your older brother got to be so good at it?"

"You mean *you* taught Mel to play? Then how come—" Foster stopped, confused.

"How come I never taught you? Because you made it pretty clear you weren't interested in any help from me."

As his father strode toward the house, Foster muttered, "I wasn't interested in being yelled at. In being called a fool every time I made a mistake."

"Heads up, Foss!"

This time the ball was coming right to him, and Foster was rewarded by the solid slap it made in Mel's mitt. Carefully, he aimed the ball at a point half a dozen feet ahead of Ricky. He was so surprised to see his little brother run forward and catch it that he barely heard Evelyn call them to dinner. Frowning, Foster wondered why *he* couldn't catch like that.

As they were finishing the meal, Mom said, "You boys have been out there practicing your baseball skills almost every day this week. It must run in the family."

"You mean 'cause Mel was captain of the high school team?" Ricky asked, his mouth mustached with milk.

She nodded. "Because of that, and because your father played semipro ball for a couple of years."

A shocked silence followed her words as everyone stared at Mr. Simmons.

"Now, why did you have to bring that up, Ruby? Not that I see any reason why it should leave them all speechless."

"It's just that it's hard to imagine you—well, it's hard to imagine you *playing*," Evelyn said.

Mom said, "Let me find my photograph album so you won't have to imagine it." She put her napkin on the table as she stood up.

"Sit down, Ruby," Father said sharply. "You know how I feel about dragging up the past. Besides, these kids aren't interested in looking at those old pictures."

"Yes, we are," the three of them chorused, and Foster wondered whether his father's flush was anger or embarrassment. When Mrs. Simmons came back, they crowded around her to look at the album none of them had known existed.

Ricky pointed to a newspaper photograph of a smiling young man and asked, "Is that really Father?"

"What does the caption say?" his mother asked.

"'Horace Simmons leads Slammers to another victory,'" Evelyn read. "And look how many of these articles there are!" she exclaimed, turning page after page until she reached a large glossy print of her father in his baseball uniform. "He was really good looking, wasn't he?" Evelyn said.

"That's 'cause he was smiling," Ricky said, and Foster realized with a jolt that he couldn't remember the last time he'd seen his father smile. The closest he ever came to it was to stop scowling. Father wasn't scowling now, Foster noticed, but he still didn't look anything like the relaxed young man in the picture.

"He looks awfully pleased with himself here," Evelyn said, bending closer to study a snapshot of a young couple. "That's you with him, isn't it, Mom?"

Mrs. Simmons nodded. "That was taken on our honeymoon. We—"

But Ricky broke in and said, "I want to see some more baseball pictures."

"That's all there are," Father said. "Grown men with family responsibilities don't play games. I'm going to read the paper."

After he left, the rest of them pored over the snapshots as Mrs. Simmons slowly turned the pages. Foster marveled at how young his parents looked. His throat ached when he saw his mother smiling down at baby Mel and then Father proudly holding a toddler dressed in a little sailor suit.

And there was Mom, holding a wide-eyed baby girl . . . Father with a tiny girl on his lap and his arm around the sturdy little boy who stood beside him. . . . A family picture now, Foster thought, peering at it. His mother stood with one arm around a little girl in a ruffled pinafore and the other around a solemn-looking school boy in short pants, and his father stood beside them, holding a blanket-wrapped baby. "Hey, that's *me*," Foster said, taking a closer look.

"Hurry up and turn the page," Ricky said. "I want to see me when I was a baby."

But when Mrs. Simmons turned the page, the next picture showed four children sitting on the bottom porch step of a farmhouse and their parents seated on the step above them. "This is the first one we have of you, Ricky," his mother said. "My folks took it while we were living with them on the farm."

Foster barely heard what she said, because he was staring at the picture of his father. The look of pride had vanished, and his face was almost expressionless.

"How come, Mom? How come you don't have a picture of me when I was a baby?" Ricky demanded.

"Times were hard for us then, Ricky, and everything your father could earn was going for necessities. There wasn't any money for extras like film."

"And then Father lost his job and we went to stay with Grandma and Grandpa," Evelyn remembered. "I loved living on the farm," she said wistfully, lingering over the pictures of the farmhouse and her grandparents.

But Father had hated it, Foster thought as his mother turned to the next page of the album and he saw the frown lines on his father's face.

"Those were difficult years for your father," Mrs.

Simmons said, and Foster noticed that in the next family picture, all the children were clustered around Mom, and Father stood a little apart from them, glaring into the camera. Mrs. Simmons turned page after page until finally she came to the one with last year's school pictures in a row at the top and this year's at the bottom.

"Wait a minute," Foster said, and he dashed to his room for the snapshot Mel had sent, the one of him standing beside the bomber. Back in the kitchen, Foster handed the picture to his mother. "Put it with our school pictures," he said, "'cause Mel was learning about flying."

"Thank you, Foster," his mother said, and she began to fit the little gummed corner pieces onto the photograph so she could mount it in the album.

Watching her, Ricky asked, "How come you never showed us these pictures before, Mom?"

"Your father doesn't like to think about the past, Rick. He doesn't want to be reminded of things that are over with now, even if they were good things."

Evelyn said flatly, "Well, I think it was wrong of him not to let you enjoy your album."

"Oh, I've enjoyed it, Evelyn. Many's the time I've taken this old book down from the closet shelf and spent an hour or so reliving those early years."

"Did you look at the baseball pictures, Mom?"

"I certainly did, Ricky."

Frowning, Evelyn asked, "Why on earth would you look at the baseball pictures?"

"Because I wanted to remember what your father was like then," she said simply. "And I'm showing the pictures to you children so you'll know that he wasn't always—well, the way he is now."

Breaking the awkward silence that followed her words, Mrs. Simmons said briskly, "Goodness, I'd better put this away or we'll never get these dishes done."

As his mother left the kitchen, Foster wondered if anyone else had noticed that there were no family pictures since they had been in California. Not a single one of all of them together, of all of them with Mel.

The next day was Saturday. Foster concentrated on throwing the ball either behind Ricky or well in front of him, and then throwing it to the left or right, trying not to wish he were doing something else. There wasn't anything else to do, Foster reminded himself. The radio programs they listened to were over hours ago, Vic's mother had taken him and Sandy to visit relatives, and it was too soon to show up at Jenny's house again.

Foster was glad for the break when Ricky saw Evelyn coming down the street and ran toward her, calling, "Hey, Evelyn! What's in the bag—is it something for me?"

"It's something for the whole family," Evelyn said.

"Let's see," Foster said, his eyes on the package she was carrying. To his surprise, she pulled out first a box of film and then an album. He frowned and said, "But there's still blank pages in the old one."

Looking mysterious, Evelyn said, "There won't be when I'm through with it."

"I want to watch, okay, Evelyn? Okay?" Ricky clamored.

"*Okay*, Ricky. You can both watch," she said, glancing at Foster.

She was up to something, and she didn't want to be caught at it alone, he thought as he followed her inside.

"You get Mom's album off her closet shelf, Foster, and Ricky, you bring me some paste and a ruler," Evelyn said. She paused in the living room doorway and added, "We'll work in the kitchen."

Foster hesitated just outside his parent's room. Mom had taught them to respect closed doors, but did closets count? And then he saw that the album was on his mother's dresser. She must have been looking at his picture of Mel, Foster thought.

He hurried to the kitchen with the album, but he stopped short when he saw what was on the table beside the supplies Ricky had found. "What are you going to do with those?" he asked, his voice hushed as he pointed to the Purple Heart and the certificate that had accompanied it. The letter from Mel's commanding officer was there, too.

"I'm dismantling that shrine on the table by Father's chair," Evelyn said. And fitting a photo mount on each corner of the letter, she stuck it onto the page opposite the school pictures. Then she attached the certificate to the next blank page and said, "Now for the medal."

"Wait a minute," Foster objected. "It's going to stick up so far the album won't close right, and it'll mess up the certificate, too."

But Evelyn said, "Just watch." And to Foster's amazement, she set the Purple Heart in the middle of the page and drew a neat square around it. Then she took a sharp knife from a drawer and cut deeply along the lines, removing a half-inch-thick block from the center of the pages that remained in the album.

"You made a cubbyhole for Mel's medal!" Ricky exclaimed.

Evelyn nodded and said, "Now if you and Foster will paste all the cut pages together to make a solid frame for the medal, this album will be filled and we can start the new one."

"How come you're going to leave us to finish this?" Foster asked suspiciously.

"Didn't you hear me say I had to take some sugar over to Barb's so she and her mom can bake cookies for the canteen?"

Foster hadn't heard that, but he wasn't sure his sister hadn't said it, so he called after her, "Just make sure you're back here by the time Father comes home." And then he turned to Ricky and said, "Look in Mom's sewing basket and bring me a piece of that white satin she used for my armband." It seemed a long time since he'd worn that armband and pretended to be the neighborhood leader of Youth for the War Effort, Foster thought as he began to paste. "Bring the scissors, too, Rick," he called as he worked.

When Ricky came back, Foster carefully cut out a square of satin and pinned the Purple Heart medal onto it. Next he pasted the satin inside the back cover of the album, and finally he spread paste all around it and pressed the back of the pasted-together pages against it. "How's that?" he asked.

"Good," Ricky said. "Mel would like it."

But would Father? Foster felt a chill. And what was Mom going to say when she saw what they'd done to her album? He was wishing he'd never let the Evil Lynn involve him in her plan when his mother came back from the hospital.

"Hel-lo-o! Anybody home?"

Foster called, "Ricky and I are in the kitchen," and at once he heard his mother's footsteps approaching.

"I see you're looking at the album again," she said, sinking into a chair and untying her shoes.

247

"Wait till you see what Foster did, Mom," Ricky said excitedly before Foster could reply. "Show her, Foster, show her."

His mouth dry, Foster opened the album to show the certificate and the Purple Heart on its bed of satin. He heard his mother catch her breath, and he didn't dare look up.

"It was Evelyn's idea, but she asked me to help. She bought a new album and some film, too. She's gone over to her friend's house but she'll be back by the time Father comes home." Foster couldn't think of anything more to say, so he waited for his mother's reaction.

After what seemed like a long time, Mrs. Simmons said slowly, "We just might be able to make this work." The two boys followed her to the living room and watched while she moved the framed picture of Mel in his uniform from the table by Father's chair to the bookcase by the radio. "Now, where are the things Evelyn brought?" she asked.

Ricky ran to get them, and his mother put the album and the box of film on top of the mail Foster had brought in earlier.

"You think he's going to be mad, Mom?" Foster asked.

"I hope not. But if he is, it certainly won't be the first time, and it won't be the last time, either, will it?"

It was easy for her to say that, Foster thought. All she'd done was move the photograph.

"Come on, Foss, let's go back out and play ball, okay?"

"Okay," Foster said, and with one last look at the photograph of Mel, he followed his little brother outside.

It seemed like hours before Ricky called, "Here comes Father. Throw me a long one so he can see how good I am."

Foster looked at a spot above Ricky's head and let the ball fly. He sensed rather than heard Father stop beside him to watch. "So. You paid some attention to what I told you," Father said, making it sound like an accusation. Foster nodded. He held his breath and hoped that this time of all times Ricky would catch the ball.

Yes! Foster wondered if Mel had felt the same satisfaction when *he* finally did something right. And then he heard his mother call. "Horace! Come see what Evelyn bought for you!"

"Bought for me? It's not my birthday again already, is it?" He looked gratified when Ricky doubled up with laughter, and then he glanced down at Foster.

Foster summoned up a wan smile and said, "It's just something Evelyn thought you'd like. She went out and got it for you today."

At the door, Mrs. Simmons gave her husband a kiss on the cheek and led him into the living room. "Look," she said, pointing to the box of film, "now you can take pictures of us all and start this new album."

"New album? We haven't used up the old one. And where's—"

But Mrs. Simmons didn't let him finish. "And there's more, Horace. Look here."

He brushed her away and said, "I don't want to look here. I want to know where you put Mel's Purple Heart."

Foster wished he could disappear. He should have known better than to let the Evil Lynn involve him in her plan. He raised anguished eyes and saw his mother opening the old album.

"It's right here, Horace," she said, lightly touching his arm. "I told you there was more. Look what the boys have done for you."

Silently, Foster cried, It's all Evelyn's fault!

Father stared from the Purple Heart medal nestled on its white satin background to the certificate on the facing page. "You say the boys—Foster and Rick—did this—for me?"

"Foster did most of it, Father, but I helped," said Ricky. "I helped him. I got the white satin from Mom's sewing basket."

"And I've moved Mel's picture onto the bookcase where we can all see it," Mom went on. "I thought I might set out my parents' wedding picture, too, and I have a frame that would fit that glossy shot of you in your baseball uniform, if you don't mind my taking it out of the album."

Father looked dazed. "I don't mind," he said.

"That's settled, then," Mom said. "Mercy, where has the time gone? You'll have to hurry if you're going to change your clothes before dinner, Horace."

When Father headed for the bedroom, Mrs. Simmons closed her eyes for a moment and drew a deep breath, and Foster realized that she had been more worried about Father's reaction than she would admit. But all she said was, "Wash your hands so you can set the table, boys."

Foster had just put a hot pad for the casserole in front of Father's place when the kitchen door opened and Evelyn came in. "It's about time you got here, you coward," he said.

But his mother shushed him. "I don't know how you thought of that, dear, but it worked," she said, giving her daughter a hug.

"I just had to do something," Evelyn said, her voice shaking. "Every time I went in the living room I'd see that Purple Heart and feel just like I did when you showed me the telegram. I want to remember Mel alive!"

Foster stared at the floor. He wanted Mel to *be* alive.

"Here comes Father," Ricky said in a loud whisper just as Mr. Simmons came into the kitchen.

"What's the matter with her?" he asked, stopping short and gesturing to Evelyn.

Evelyn wiped the tears from her cheek and said, "I'm glad you liked the album, Father."

"Yes, it's very nice." After he sat down, Father asked, "Ruby, if I can find the camera, do you think the old man next door would be willing to take a picture of us after church tomorrow when we're all presentable?" He looked pointedly at Foster's shorts.

"These are patriotic stains, Father," Foster said, sliding into his place at the table. "I got them picking berries for the war effort."

Father rolled his eyes and muttered, "Patriotic stains, now. What excuse will he come up with next?"

Foster grinned across the table at his sister, and it wasn't until she bowed her head that he realized his father was saying grace. Foster had gotten so used to clasping hands around the table and singing a blessing that he'd almost forgotten the way things had been before they found out Mel was missing.

Suddenly Foster realized that his father had added something to his usual grace. What was that he'd said? Something about blessing this family. Could they ever be a real family? A family like the ones he read about where everyone—

"*Fos*ter!"

"Huh? Could I please have another serving of— Oh." Embarrassed, Foster reached for the plate his father was handing him and passed it on to his brother, then took his own plate and settled it in front of him. Macaroni and cheese had been Mel's favorite. Would he remember that every time he ate it for the rest of his life? And if he did, would it always make him feel empty inside instead of just hungry?

A jab from Ricky's elbow brought another "Huh?" from Foster.

"You haven't touched your dinner, dear," Mom repeated. "Is anything wrong?"

He shook his head and began to eat, surprised at the comfort the warm, soft, cheesy noodles brought him. Not as wrong as it used to be, anyway, he thought, silently answering his mother's question.

CHAPTER
27

Foster sat on the front porch while Ricky and Sandy marched up and down the sidewalk waving small American flags. They had been shouting "Hup! Two, three, four!" over and over again for what seemed like an hour, and Foster wondered if he would have found that fun when he was Ricky's age. He didn't think so.

Nothing was much fun now. He couldn't think of a single thing he wanted to do, and he'd never had that problem before. Not before Mel died.

Someone called his name, and Foster saw Vic coming across the street with a bulging knapsack.

"Here's all the stuff you lent me," Vic said, lowering it to the ground with a thump. "My mom said I should bring it back now that we don't play the war game anymore."

"You don't play the war game?" Foster echoed. "How come?"

Vic shrugged. "It just wasn't the same. After Pam and Jenny quit, it was mostly just the younger kids, and—"

"The girls quit? Why?"

"Well, Jenny said we ought to stop for a week out of respect for you, because of your brother, and then Pam made one of her speeches. You know how she is. Anyway, by the time she was through—'blah, blah, blah, and war isn't a game, you know, and blah, blah, blah,'—nobody felt much like playing. I don't care, 'cause it wasn't all that much fun after you left."

After General Foster Simmons left the battleground, his demoralized troops lost the will to fight. A truce was declared, and— "Huh?"

"You're not going to be like that again, are you?"

"Like what?"

"You know. Always out in left field."

Foster stared at Vic, shocked by the note of scorn he'd heard in the other boy's voice. Thinking quickly, he asked, "Speaking of left field, did you know my father used to play semipro ball?"

"Yeah, sure."

Foster got to his feet and said, "Wait here, and I'll prove it to you."

The two boys were still reading the clippings in the album when Mrs. Simmons came home from her day at the hospital. She opened her purse and handed Foster a notice.

"'Junior Red Cross Seeking Volunteers,'" he read. "Volunteers for what?"

"One of the other nurses' aides told me her son helps

assemble the keyboard sets servicemen use to practice Morse code, and her little girl helps make up packages to send to the boys overseas."

Almost in unison, Foster and Vic asked, "How old is her son?"

"About your age, I think."

Foster's eyes strayed to Ricky. Was his brother old enough to help make up the packages?

"Hey, Foss," Vic said, looking up from the notice, "it says here they're opening a new summer volunteer center next week, and its going to be at our school!"

Maybe Ricky could play on the playground if he was too young to volunteer, Foster thought, his interest growing. "After supper, let's go tell all the kids," he said.

The boys were so involved with their plans that they didn't notice Mr. Simmons until he stopped in front of them. "What's my album doing out here?" he demanded. "And what's that mess?"

"Foster was showing me the baseball articles," Vic said, quickly getting to his feet. "I never knew you used to play ball!"

"I'll put everything away," Foster said, picking up the album and the knapsack and escaping into the house. When he came back, Father had set down his lunch box and was swinging an imaginary bat while Vic watched and listened intently.

After Mr. Simmons went inside, Vic said accusingly,

"How come you never told me your father played semi-pro ball?"

Foster shrugged. He couldn't very well admit that he hadn't known.

On Monday morning, Foster and Vic signed their names on the volunteer register, and a smiling woman handed them each a sleeve patch.

"Almost as good as that armband you had for the YWE, isn't it?" Vic said as he ran his finger over the red cross on a shield centered in the circular patch. "What ever became of the YWE, anyhow?"

"I guess there isn't much need for it anymore," Foster said vaguely. "Look, here come Michael and Wilbur."

A short time later, the boys were busy assembling stretchers, and after his initial disappointment that he wouldn't be making Morse code keyboards, Foster found that he enjoyed the work, especially sanding the wooden handles to make them smooth.

"Wouldn't want our medics to get splinters, now, would we?" asked the elderly volunteer who was overseeing the workers. "Any of you boys have fathers or brothers in the service?"

As the hands shot up around him, Foster focused all his attention on his work. He wished he had a sleeve patch with a gold star on it, so people would know without asking, know that he was a "Gold Star Brother," as Ricky would say.

It seemed no time at all before it was noon and everyone headed home for lunch. Mom was right, Foster thought as he went to meet Ricky. Keeping busy did help.

CHAPTER
28

Foster's breath came so hard he thought his chest would burst, but making one last effort he jumped up and whammed the tetherball with all his strength. It unwound so fast that Vic's cry of triumph turned into a yelp and he leaped backward. Foster slugged the ball again and again, as again and again Vic swung at it and missed.

He was doing it. He was going to win! Panting, Foster stood back and watched the rope wind around the top few inches of the pole until the ball was tight against it and he heard Ricky cheer.

"Good game, Foss," Vic said grudgingly. "You finally got the hang of it."

"Yeah, finally," Foster said, trying not to sound as pleased as he felt.

And then Ricky was tugging at his arm and saying, "It's almost dark, Foss—we'd better go."

"See you tomorrow, Vic," Foster called. He turned to

his brother, who was trying to pull him toward home, and said, "Lay off, Ricky—it's not all that late."

When they came into the house, Father called to them from the living room. "Make sure you two are here when I get home from work tomorrow, you understand?"

The boys nodded silently, and while they were refilling their water glasses at the kitchen sink, Ricky whispered, "You don't think he wants to play ball with us, do you?"

"I hope not," Foster whispered back. Maybe if he worked at it, he could be almost as good a big brother as Mel had been, but no matter how hard he tried or how much he practiced, he would never be anywhere near as good a ballplayer. . . .

The next afternoon, Foster and Ricky set up the Monopoly game on Mel's bed and took their places on either side of the board. At least it was a change from baseball, Foster thought.

Much later, a car door slammed, and Ricky ran to the window. "It's him, Foss—it's him."

"We'd better get out there," Foster said. He wondered what had been so important that Father had driven to work in spite of the fact that his worn tires had to last for the duration.

The boys were outside before their father reached the porch. "You two bring in that box on the backseat while I look at the mail," he said.

Reluctantly, Foster followed Ricky to the car, hoping Father hadn't bought something else from "Mr. Black." He hadn't seemed this pleased with himself since he'd brought home all that sugar.

"Read what it says, Foss! Read what it says," Ricky urged, almost falling over his own feet in his eagerness for his brother to see what was in the car. "You think that's really what's in there? Do you?"

The box was labeled LIONEL TRAINS, and the contents shifted with a clank when Foster pulled it toward him. His heartbeat quickened.

"It *is* a train set, isn't it?" Ricky said, hardly able to contain himself.

The boys were struggling toward the house with the box when Father came out and said, "I wondered what was keeping you two. Here, I'll carry that."

They ran ahead to open the door, then followed their father down the hall to their room, where he set the box on the floor. He tossed Foster the car keys and said, "Get the other box out of the trunk, and make sure you don't lose my keys, you hear me?"

Foster raced for the car. The square box in the trunk was big, but it wasn't heavy like the other one had been. He was halfway to the house before he realized he'd left the key in the trunk lock, and he set the box down and dashed back to the curb.

Ricky was reverently holding a shining gray engine in both hands when Foster came into the bedroom, and he could see the name COMMODORE VANDERBILT in black letters on its side. Craning his neck he saw a yellow flat car, a silvery Sunoco tank car, and a red caboose still in the open box. He barely noticed Father taking the other box from him and opening it, but Ricky did.

"Look here, Foss—little trees, with snow on them! And houses and— Hey, it's a whole town!" Ricky lifted out the trees and buildings one by one and lined them up at the foot of Mel's bed.

Foster was still staring into the first box, transfixed by the sight of what looked to him like miles and miles of track sections. "This is the best train set I ever saw," he said. "How did you get it?"

"Bought it from a man at work whose son just joined the navy. The kid figured that instead of letting it go for scrap, he'd sell it and put the money toward a war bond. You like it, huh?"

Foster nodded. He couldn't remember Father ever giving him and Ricky anything before, giving them something for no reason at all. Especially something like this. How could anyone have even thought of discarding it as scrap? Foster was kneeling by the box, examining the miniature lantern that could be hooked up to flash red and green, when his mother came home.

"Well, it looks like the three of you have your work cut out for you if you're going to set that up this evening," she said. "I'll change out of my uniform and help you dismantle that bed so you'll have room for the track."

Foster felt as though his hands were frozen to the engine he was holding, and Ricky cried, "Mel's bed? You're going to take away Mel's bed?"

"Mel doesn't need it anymore, honey," Mrs. Simmons said quietly, "but someone who's come here to find a job in the shipyards could use it. I think Mel would want some young American working hard for his country to have a comfortable place to rest at the end of a shift, don't you?"

Ricky nodded and began to move the little trees and buildings from the bed to his bunk. "Mel would want us to have room to set up the train set Father brought us, too," he said.

"I wish I were six years old so I could be distracted that easily," Foster muttered as he began to put away the Monopoly game they had abandoned. He didn't realize anyone had heard him until a choked voice came from behind him.

"So do I, Foster. So do I."

Foster felt a hand brush his shoulder, and mouth open, he watched his father leave the room.

"Are you mad at me, Foss? Mad at me for letting them take away Mel's bed?"

Foster turned to his younger brother, and when he saw the worried look on Ricky's face he shook his head.

"Mom's right. Mel doesn't need it, and somebody else can use it." He thought of all the "Wanted: Room to Rent" ads pinned to the bulletin board at church and remembered the notice about the Ladies' Circle collecting used furniture for newly arrived families. Suddenly it seemed selfish to keep an empty bed. "And I think you're right, too," Foster added, "right that Mel would want us to have room to set up the train."

Mrs. Simmons looked up when Foster came into the kitchen and asked her, "Mom, do you think he got that for us 'cause Evelyn bought him the album?"

His mother shook her head, and Evelyn asked, "Got you what?"

After Foster had described the train set, Evelyn's eyes filled with tears and she said, "Mel would have loved that when he was a kid. Every year at Christmas he was so sure he was going to get a Lionel train set, and he never did, and now those two get it. It's not fair!"

Foster was stunned. "Is that why he got it for us?"

But Mrs. Simmons had turned to her daughter. "You're right, Evelyn," she said, "it's not fair. The Depression wasn't fair, and God knows this war isn't fair, and your father couldn't do a thing about either one of them. But now that he's making good money and has his debts paid off, one thing he *can* do is buy a train set for Foster and Ricky. I think Mel would be happy for them, and for his father, too. Can't you see how important this is for Horace, Evelyn?"

Important for Father? Foster frowned. His father had seemed—well, not happy, exactly, but—

Suddenly, Foster was aware of someone whistling. The tune stopped when Mr. Simmons came into the kitchen and saw that Ricky wasn't at the table. "Rick!" he shouted. "You get yourself in here right now!"

Ricky came charging into the kitchen, and Father demanded, "Don't you know better than to run in the house? And have you washed your hands?"

Ricky nodded as he slipped into his seat.

"Don't you lie to me, Richard Simmons," Father said, his voice deadly quiet.

"He means he knows better than to run in the house," Foster said quickly, adding, "Go wash your hands, Ricky." His brother made a wide detour around the table, and Foster said, "He's just excited about the train set, Father. It isn't every day a kid gets something like that."

"Well, he still has to come to the table on time," Father said, but he sounded mollified.

"Why?"

Suddenly all eyes were on Evelyn, and she cleared her throat and said, "I asked why it's so important for Ricky to be here precisely on time."

"I punch a time clock every day, young lady, and so does everyone else at the plant. It's never too soon to learn the importance of being prompt."

Drawing courage from his sister, Foster said, "I think

Ricky's already learned that. He wasn't late for school once all year, and he's always ready when it's time for us to leave for church."

"What is this, anyway?" Father said, looking from Foster to Evelyn. "What do you two think gives you the right to question—"

"There you are, Ricky," Mrs. Simmons said brightly as the little boy came back into the kitchen. "Sit down, dear, so your father can ask the blessing."

Father glared down the table at his wife, and she said quietly, "This isn't an aircraft factory, Horace. This is our home."

From the corner of his eye, Foster saw his father's fisted hands begin to relax, saw him bow his head to ask the blessing.

Foster raised his eyes at Father's "amen," and beside him, Ricky whispered, "Hurry, so we can set up the track."

Father said gruffly, "Sounds like you fellows think that train set's all right."

"It's a great set, Father," Foster said. "We're really glad you got it for us."

And Ricky echoed, "It's a great set, Father," and then he whispered, "Hurry up, Foss."

A few minutes later, Foster gestured to his clean plate and asked, "May Ricky and I please be excused?"

"Of course," his mother said, "as long as your sister

doesn't mind doing your share of the after-dinner chores this once."

To Foster's amazement, Evelyn shook her head and said, "I don't mind." She had really changed, Foster thought as he followed Ricky out of the kitchen. He might even have to stop thinking of her as the Evil Lynn.

"Listen, Foster," Ricky said the minute they were in their room, "you don't think Father's going to come in here to help us set up this track, do you?"

Remembering that faintest of touches on his shoulder, Foster said, "He's going to help us, Ricky, 'cause if he doesn't come in here on his own, we're going to find him and ask him to."

"But maybe he won't want to help."

"He'll want to." When Foster saw his brother's face fall, he ruffled the younger boy's hair and said, "It will be okay, Ricky—honest. You'll see."

ABOUT THE AUTHOR

Carolyn Reeder is an acclaimed author of historical fiction for young people. Her first novel, *Shades of Gray*, won the Scott O'Dell Award and the Jefferson Cup, both given for outstanding historical fiction. *Shades of Gray* was also named an ALA Notable Children's Book and was selected as an Honor Book for the Jane Addams Children's Book Award, and it received the Child Study Association Award. Like her next two novels, *Grandpa's Mountain* and *Moonshiner's Son*, it is on numerous state master reading lists.

A former reading teacher and an all-the-time history buff, Carolyn Reeder lives in Maryland with her husband.